Guardian Harmony

If wishes were fishes

Written by
Katelynn Alexandrea

This book is routinely laughed at by the interdimensional covens of Seawitches, everywhere, and Leftenant Karina Gill does not appreciate it.

For Dr. Zeidler,

The *other* good doctor Z(My favorite real life magicless sea witch who saves lives).

For Mom,

With special thanks for the best medicine, growing up; 3 AM reruns of Columbo, Perry Mason, and Magnum P.I..

And of course,

Raymond Burr, Peter Falk, Tom Selleck, Carolyne Keene, Franklin Dixon, David Robbins, Mark Harmon, Brian Bendis and Micheal Gaydos, Hans Christian Andersen, The brothers Grimm, Tolkein, and Charles Perrault. The faces, and authors without whom my love for writing would not be.

Not to mention…

Folgers, Maxwell house, Nabob, The Full Throttle Energy drink company, Coca-cola, and ~~Starbucks~~Sharkbucks.

We'd all have filet mignon.

(Dean Koontz version)

If you're curious about the other half of the idiom that the title came from, that's one version of it. There are countless other versions of this saying, and that is sort of the point of only using the first part of the saying.

This book had a lot of strange inspirations, really strange lore books to dreams I can't explain(except that one dream about meeting Harmony in a bar. That one's explainable. I'm gay.), to an errant thought my brain had, while trying to come to terms with a local disease outbreak.

As to the traditional thank you's that go in the forward of these books, I'd like to thank Doctor Z, my personal fairy godmother, and my mother, younger sister, daughter, and daughter's mother for being supportive in my quest to have my wish granted. I love you all beyond words.

And some additional thanks;

Jessie, for introducing me to Ketchup(the proper noun), Nookmiles and 5 or 6 other things that confuse my spellcheck. Thank you for the light you bring. It has meant, and will mean more than I have words for.

Cass, my previous cover artist. Words are not enough to explain how much I care and hope you are okay.

C.K. Books, whose fantastic work on this cover was worth every penny. You can commission artwork from them at https://ckbookcoverdesigns.com

Lady J, Rule 8. Thank you for being here.

Ellie(And Pixie), Carly(And Carly, you two can argue about who goes first), Marcus, Jessi, *also Jessi*, Jess, *also Jessie*, Jessy, *also Jessy*, Jen, *also Jen*, Lexie, *also Lexie*, Quish, Bob, Sephi, Pengy, Sunshine, and Juffy. Life would not be the same without you, and I love you all.

John, Revke, and Bert, whose help, support, and John's weekly writer's chat have helped recharge my writing muses after they took a hit.

Lexi, Amber, and Terril for introducing me to perspectives that helped my own life make sense.

The other J, thanks for everything(and it was a *LOT* of everything to thank you for).

And of course,

You, for buying this book.

May you get what you wish for, and survive what it costs you. You've survived worse than this.

Prologue
March 14th, 2020

Barb & Cecil

I always tried my best to have March 14th booked off. It was an unwritten rule. I took some leave time.

It was the same routine. I would stay with Granddad. He didn't live far off base. We would talk about those we lost. Those we served with. Those we loved.

Like mom. Like Lauren.

Lauren was a touchy subject with Granddad. He didn't like talking about his once and never again great grandchild. Without my mother's advice, caring for an infant partly Rusalka child was difficult and she had died of pneumonia while I was deployed and she was in his care.

It was a dark subject. We rarely broached it. It was painful and while I knew he blamed himself, I no more blamed him, than I did my mother. I blamed myself. It was 14 years ago, by now. I had been in Iraq. Involuntary deployment with no special circumstances about my child taken into account. Sometimes the system worked. Sometimes it didn't. A contract, however, is a contract. Children don't change that.

Today was the day we talked about her as we sat in what was once my and then her bedroom. The empty cradle was still there.

Granddad sat on the bed.

I sat on mom's old rocking chair.

And we drank. Real vodka. Undiluted. For Granddad, that was harder than it was for me. He was in his 90's, after all.

And we talked.

This year, though, something was different.

There was a foldout chair in the corner and a bottle of tequila on hand.

"So." Granddad spoke only a touch above a whisper. "That's... the great family shame."

Leftenant Alyssa Sanchez did not offer an accusing look at either of us. She just sat back, watching us both, sipping her tequila.

"Do the others know?" Alyssa asked, speaking up for the first time in hours.

I shook my head. "No." It was a one word answer that spoke many in tone.

"For the same reason they didn't know you were Rusalka." Alyssa squinted. "Not because you didn't trust them. Because you didn't want more pain."

"She's good." Granddad nodded. "We hang the phone off the receiver. Cell phones are turned off. We don't answer the door. My side of the family is insistent upon sending condolences. We don't want to feel anyone else's second hand regret. We've got enough of our own. We don't need the big idiot, or that sweet girl making it worse, either."

Alyssa nodded and quietly went downstairs for a moment. She returned with a white box. "In my family, we have a tradition of mourning. We call it cake day." Alyssa nodded, opening the box. "I prefer brownies, but they're not traditional. Guppy is lactose and gluten intolerant, so instead, we have vegan gluten free chocolate cake."

"You can get that?" Granddad asked, looking in the box.

"There's this chain that started out as prepared, ready to cook all natural and healthy meats. Now, they're all about Real Food, as they put it, and about a quarter of their store is gluten free. About half the deserts." Alyssa nodded, handing him the box. "Chocolate releases happy chemicals in your brain. It helps numb out the parts of your brain overwhelmed by sad memories and lets you grieve in a healthier way that doesn't feel like a sad, hopeless pit you can't get out of."

"That sounds like a lot of mumbo jumbo to excuse eating an entire cake by yourself." Granddad narrowed his eyes.

"There are four of us." Alyssa retorted with a fake offended expression.

I took one of the slices from the box. It was gooey and didn't resemble any chocolate cake I had ever seen, but this cake was different. Someone had gone to great lengths to find a cake I could eat.

I looked at it, excitedly. My nose was less excited. It smelled kind of bland, somehow. There were smells I could not identify. It suddenly became concerning.

"She's never had chocolate before?" Alyssa asked.

Granddad shook his head.

"Chocolate is usually in the realm of gluten and dairy." I nodded.

Alyssa grinned, taking a slice for herself.

"What?" I asked.

Granddad shook his head. There was a strange look on his face.

And then he snickered ever so gently.

"WHAT?" I asked.

Granddad gestured to the cake. "If that's half as good as the real real chocolate cake, you'll be an addict."

"Oh, come-" I took a bite, then spit it out onto the piece of paper towel. "GROSS!"

"*Gross*?" Granddad and Alyssa asked at the same time.

"That's just plants with bits in it." I shook my head. "That is not food."

"Huh." Alyssa blinked. "Did not see that coming."

"I should have." Granddad chuckled. "We learned at a very young age that Harmony's body was intolerant to most plants that weren't rice, potatoes, nuts, seaweed, or cranberries unless they were prepared properly and served alongside something not *vegan*." He leaned down, and withdrew a bowl with a decent sized whole salmon in it and handed it to me. "Fortunately, I wasn't expecting her to be satisfied with a bit of sugar."

Alyssa shook her head, and chuckled a bit. "Harmony will always be Harmony. She's been pretty heavily into a meat diet lately, anyway."

Granddad raised his glass of vodka at that. "You keep that in mind, you two will go a long way together."

"You don't seem that surprised by the prospect of a long-term relationship for your promiscuous siren granddaughter." Alyssa pointed out.

"I was hoping she would find the same peace her mother did, one day. I'll admit that it's unexpected, but it's a pleasant surprise and you two will not have a single comment said against you in my house." Granddad refilled his glass.

"Ah. Yes. The age old tradition. This is the family you've got. If you love them, you don't waste them." Alyssa nodded.

"Your family, too?" Granddad asked.

Alyssa shook her head. "First time I brought a girl home to mamá, she chased us out of her house with a frying pan when she found out we were dating. Told me I wasn't welcome back in her house. I found another one."

"Well, then, you have a family here, too." Granddad nodded. "There aren't many of us left. My wife and I, and Harmony's aunt Valerie." Granddad shrugged. "But this is your home now."

Alyssa shook her head.

Granddad was confused for just a second. "Ah. Fish of fin, then." He chuckled. "Stripes and spots. I see."

Alyssa gave him an uncertain look.

"This is as much your home as it is Harmony's, even though she'll inherit it eventually." Granddad nodded. "Harmony's home is out there. Wearing that uniform."

"Harmony is always going to be Harmony, and Lyssa gotta Lyssa." Alyssa nodded. "Though I will gladly call you my family, if you're okay with that. As it stands, I don't have much of that."

Granddad inclined his head. "Harmony sort of collects the misfits into her pack. The Zaheer girl, Zilla, might as well be my great granddaughter. She spent a few years here, while she did High school. She still stays here, sometimes. Barb loves that. She doesn't normally get to cook that many vegetables in one sitting, any-more. Jill has great stories about where she grew up. We've heard them all a dozen times and I hope to hear them a few dozen more. That Italian fellow, though, we don't tolerate in this house after he insulted Barb's lasagna."

Alyssa chuckled at that. "Yeah, that sounds like Harmony's mama bear instincts."

Granddad gave her an amused look. "She's a shark, young lady. Not a bear. Don't get your metaphors crossed."

Alyssa shook her head. "Not around Jill. It makes a kind of sense, now. I should have guessed the big secret. Orphan refugee girl without living parents. Guardian mother without children. Instincts take over."

Granddad looked thoughtfully towards me at that, before nodding. "It's glaringly obvious."

"You know I hate this game." I hissed.

"What game?" Granddad chuckled.

"The game where we openly discuss her psyche in front of her." Alyssa filled in. "It makes her self conscious." She added in a whisper.

"Oh, I know." Granddad laughed. "I take it that it's a commonplace thing? Her reaction is a lot less angry than it used to be."

I nodded. "Ever since I revealed myself to Vinny and Jill."

"I think it was when you met me, actually." Alyssa corrected. "That reminds me." Alyssa dug into her purse and withdrew a black file. "Do you know what this is?"

Granddad gave it a confused look before shaking his head.

Alyssa handed it to him.

"Military Intelligence." Granddad frowned. "On… you?"

I nodded. "Did dad ever talk about intelligence keeping an eye on mom?"

Granddad shook his head.

"She's in there." I added, nodding to the file.

"And how did you come by it?" Granddad asked.

"It was given freely to destroy as we see fit." Alyssa said, in a softer tone. "After we were drafted into the military intelligence branch of CFNIS."

"Ah." Granddad nodded. "The price of your services is a clean slate, then." He paused to look over the file, after putting on his reading glasses that were usually hung around his neck. "They know everything about her. And you. They know things about her that *I* don't." He paused. "And things about you, it would seem, as well."

I nodded before handing him my own folder, from my bag.

"You don't usually bring your-" Granddad stopped and raised his eyebrows at the file. "What is *Vampirizing Fasciitis*?"

"A Russian plot." Alyssa said, quietly. "We're under orders to read in any family members who the Russian intelligence folks might target in retaliation."

Granddad flipped through the file, eyes settling on the final page. "There were other Rusalka involved." He said, quietly.

I nodded.

"That must have been… something." Granddad said, shaking his head. "I'm sorry, little pup. That couldn't have been easy."

Alyssa chuckled.

"What?" Granddad asked.

"I call her Guppy." Alyssa clarified.

"Innocent as a child until provoked." Granddad nodded. "Though I imagine that this would add a few years to your soul."

"They expected me to join them." I paused. "One of them knew my mother."

Granddad frowned at that. "Then they did not know her well."

I smiled at that.

"You seem no worse for the wear, pup." Granddad said, handing the files back to us both. "I'll let your grandmother know, too. We'll step up our security."

"Thank you." I said, quietly.

"Now for the important part." Granddad said, grabbing the bouquets of flowers off the nightstand.

"Right." I agreed.

The three of us walked to the backyard. Grandma was already there.

"You took your time, Cecil." Grandma said, quietly.

"Official business came up." Granddad shrugged.

It was a family tradition. We kept our loved ones close.

There were five generations of Williams buried here. Six, counting Lauren.

Dad. Mom. Mom's grave grew strange flowers every year. So did Lauren's.

We placed flowers at both of the simple headstones with their names etched into them. Dad's had a military rank insignia, too. Half the plots here did, dating back to pre-world war one. Navy. Army. There was a pilot in world war I.

"I like this." Alyssa said, quietly, observing the plot. "It's... intimate. In its own dark way, beautiful, as well."

Granddad nodded.

"That's what I thought the first time I saw it." Grandma nodded.

The gate on the side of the house opened and closed with a loud creak.

Alyssa, Granddad, and I all drew our pistols in the exact same way, and Grandma held up her cane, threateningly.

No scary Russian spies, though. No assassins.

Just a young woman in uniform, rolling up in a wheelchair.

My nostrils flared at the scent of her, almost in fear at first, before realizing something wasn't right.

She held up a Military Intelligence ID. "Leftenant Karina Gill. I'm looking for Commander Williams? She's not answering her-" The woman paused, looking at us, and then behind us. "Ah."

"Gill." Alyssa laughed.

Granddad snorted ever so slightly.

"It gets funnier." I said, trying not to laugh, once the joke had been made obvious.

"What?" The woman asked. "What's so funny to you?"

"She smells like a merperson." I said, calmly. "A Cecaelia, to be exact."

Alyssa chuckled at that.

"How do you know what merpeople *smell* like?" The Leftenant asked.

"When this penny drops, let me know. I've got to get the ramp out of the shed." Granddad laughed.

"The ramp?" Karina asked.

"Dad lost his legs in Desert Storm. We have a more or less wheel-chair accessible first floor." I clarified.

"How do you know what I am?" Karina demanded.

"I also know you aren't a sea witch." I added, giving Alyssa an amused look.

Karina's face contorted into a seriously confused frown.

I bared webbed fingers, claws, and siren teeth. "Hello, squidgirl." I said, in an amused tone.

Karina looked startled, and fell out of her wheelchair.

"Hey! Easy!" Alyssa said, hastily moving to help her back in. "Easy. It's okay. Harmony's not going to eat you."

"So they *didn't* tell you anything about me." I said, raising an eyebrow.

Karina shook her head.

"Come on, inside." Alyssa chuckled. "We've got some gluten free vegan chocolate cake."

"And Coffee. Police food is probably better tasting than that cake." Granddad added, placing a large ramp on the ground over the cement back stairs. "Don't dawdle. It's going to storm soon. My hip hates the storms."

"Then why live in *Vancouver*?" Karina shouted after him, which only provoked a hearty chuckle.

I gestured for Karina to go first.

"That was mean, Guppy."

"That was a test, Lyssa. She passed."

"Ah."

Karina

Karina sat awkwardly at the table while Grandma set it with cups of coffee, and tea. She held up a tea pot and coffee cup.

"What'll it be, for you, dear?" Grandma asked.

"Coffee, please. With a bit of sugar." Karina said, quietly. "I'm in so much trouble. I should have listened to Chief Petty Officer Zaheer."

"Yes." Alyssa nodded. "You should have. You're here now."

"You're not in danger, little fish. Calm down." I added, in a more soothing tone. "Eat. Drink. We don't hurt innocent people in this family, you just chose a bad day to drop in."

"Oh." Karina looked relieved.

"You're a sea witch." Granddad looked confused. "Why are you so afraid of guns?"

"Cecaelia." My tone switched to chastisement. "They're not one and the same. Other merpeople can be sea witches. Cecaelia don't always have magic. She doesn't have the danger magic smell."

"What's with the wheelchair?" Grandma asked. "Did you serve already?"

"And now. In case you missed the rank insignias on my uniform. " Karina nodded. "Can't really discuss it with civilians. It was a classified operation. Long story short, they pulled most of the shrapnel out of my spine, but on land or under water, my lower extremities don't function. Spinal cord damage."

"So even as a Cecaelia." Alyssa squinted. "You can't swim?"

Karina nodded.

"No magic. No legs. No tentacles." I shook my head. "Yet, you work for intelligence. That must mean you're one hell of an intelligence officer, to overcome all of that."

Karina cleared her throat, before handing me a file. "Your eyes only."

I looked it over, raising my eyebrows. "Who even speaks Latin anymore?" I asked.

"Or Serbian. I get that a lot." Karina said, with a nod.

"People from Serbia, presumably." Grandma noted, dryly.

I handed the file back to her. "Why do I need this?"

"Read the front of the folder, Guppy. That's an assignment order dossier." Alyssa pointed.

"A what?" I blinked.

"I'm being assigned to your team as an intelligence analyst." Karina put the file back in my hands. "So read that. It might save your life one day."

"Guppy isn't one for reading." Alyssa chuckled. "She's more instinctive."

"I've heard." Karina nodded. "Though I just now got the joke."

Grandma placed some food out and I took one of the chicken drumsticks, happily crunching clean through it, bone and all.

Karina gave me an open mouthed stare.

"You're wondering where the chicken bones go." Alyssa laughed.

"How-" Karina frowned.

"Rusalka thing. She needs the bones to grow and repair her own bones. She's lactose intolerant. Gotta get calcium somewhere. It's also a *fantastic* party trick." Alyssa explained. "She ate an entire chicken last week. Freaked the base commander right out."

"*Rusalka*?" Karina's stare deepened. "I never thought I'd meet one, and live to tell the tale."

"In fairness, most Rusalka prefer to meet people by spelling meet as E-A-T." I chuckled.

Karina took a moment. "Well, I met this Lamia once when I was in I-can't-tell-you-istan. They're quite similar. I imagine her metabolism is a lot slower, but she got her bone mass from digesting other bones. She was nice. For a Lamia. I can't imagine if you were a homicidal merperson, they'd let you live very long, let alone hold a respected Navy rank."

"Oh, good." Granddad smiled. "She can use her brain." He added, placing a slice of cake in front of her.

"I'm sorry for intruding. This case is… personal. I can't really talk about it much here, but I'm worried people are in danger." Karina said, quietly. "And intelligence assigned me to you. I'm guessing you're the one they expect to get this resolved."

"Must be something weird then." Alyssa tilted her head. "They told us we might occasionally come across… unusual cases."

"We ain't spring chickens, honey, but we ain't stupid in this house." Grandma added.

Karina gave her a perplexed look.

"You're worried for the same reason Harmony was worried about the last case." Alyssa filled in the blanks.

"Last case?" Karina looked even more perplexed.

I reached into my bag. "I'll trade you files. Let's get you up to date."

Karina raised her eyebrows at the file. "Why do you have this off base?"

"Orders." Alyssa clarified. "We're supposed to read in any family that might be threatened in response to the case being resolved as it was."

Karina gave her a raised eyebrow before reading on, then raising the other after a couple pages. "Ink." She said, quietly. "What a mess." She gave a disapproving stare. "And you consider this dolphin scat a *properly closed case*?"

"Is Alyssa right?" I asked.

"To an extent." Karina nodded.

"Is Ink a swear word? Like how Harmony says fish hooks?" Alyssa asked.

Karina gave her a glare.

"She likes to analyze people. You get used to it." I shrugged. "Or maybe I do, because we sleep together. I should ask Vinny."

"Vinny does NOT like it." Alyssa said, dryly. "That's half the reason I do it. Jill eggs me on."

"Jill would. Such a sweet girl." Grandma said, in a delighted tone. "Well, I suppose that's your leave cancelled, isn't it?"

I frowned, but nodded. "You know the drill."

"For Queen and Country." Granddad nodded. "Good luck, you two. I expect you all to be in this house again. You can bring your eight legged friend, if she's staying around."

"Technically a tentacle is neither an arm, nor a leg." Karina pointed out.

"And technically, squid, unlike octopi, do not have a generic number of them. Different species have different numbers." I added.

"Oh, delightful." Granddad laughed. "She's a 'technically' girl. She's definitely welcome back. I love the fun conversations where we pick apart the exacting syntax of things, while explaining them. Leftenant Sanchez is better than Harmony at those."

"I could have guessed." Karina laughed. "Though, I imagine there are things she does not understand, which Commander Williams would."

"World would be boring if everybody knew everything." Grandma shrugged.

Karina nodded. "I have to get back to base, to finish my check in. I just needed Commander Williams' signature."

"Harmony." I paused, to sign the form. "Nobody calls me Commander Williams unless they outrank me. It's backwards, but you catch on. I only play at being a superior officer."

Karina looked perplexed.

"If you're on Harmony's team, you're part of Harmony's family. That's just how it works around here." Alyssa added.

Karina shook her head. "That's so... strange."

"No, dear girl." Granddad explained. "That's how it should be. So long as you make her proud, she will respect you, care about you, and lay down her life to protect you. That's who Harmony is."

"I hate this game." I chimed in.

"Wait." Karina tilted her head. "Even... someone you just met?"

"Used to be, Guppy would flirt with people she met, inside 10 seconds." Alyssa chuckled. "It doesn't matter to her. Instincts are instincts."

"She's going to trust you with her life. She's going to ask you to trust her with your own." Granddad added. "That's a kind of family that doesn't need to be blood."

"She does it freely, too." Alyssa added. "No strings, or prices. It's just how she's programmed. You're part of her school, or pod, or whatever now. Buck up, small fry. You're family whether you agree to it or not."

"Rusalka use canine terms, like sharks do. Pups. Packs." Karina shook her head. "I don't think I belong here. I'm just following orders."

"Well, that hardly matters." Alyssa shrugged. "But you do you, Morgana."

"Don't." Karina winced. "I hate that movie."

"You, too?" I asked, raising eyebrows.

"Racist and derogatory." Karina nodded.

"I could see that." Grandma nodded. "Harmony, you take care of this girl. She seems like a good person."

"Like Harmony could do anything else." Alyssa laughed.

"We should probably get back to base." I interjected. "I don't like leaving Vinny unattended with brain work."

"Not his strong suit?" Karina asked.

"Vinny is to brain work, what you are to climbing trees. He's got a job to do. Thinking ain't it." Alyssa explained.

"Ah. One of *them*." Karina nodded.

"He's not a bad person." Grandad nodded. "He's just not very pleasant, sometimes."

"And he's dumb as a bag of steer manure." Grandma added.

"Not a house for subtlety." Karina chuckled.

"No." I chuckled. "No, it's not."

"Hey, Guppy, should we…" Alyssa nodded to Karina.

"What?" I asked. "Tell the others? No. That's her choice to make, just as it was mine."

Karina looked relieved. "I appreciate that."

"I remember how terrifying it was when someone else revealed what I was to Alyssa without asking me if it was okay." I said, quietly. "*I* trust them. You have only read Intel files about them."

Alyssa nodded. "Is that better?" She asked Karina.

"Very much so." Karina took a deep breath. "Thank you."

"That's what you do." I said, placing a hand on her shoulder. "You protect those you are close to."

Karina tilted her head. "She's really taken den motherhood to heart."

"It's sweet." Alyssa nodded. "It's one of Harmony's better qualities."

"I'm scared to ask what her less good ones are." Karina winced.

"Thinking with my heart before my brain, an addiction now kept between Alyssa and myself and a fondness for mischief that gets me routinely in trouble." I shrugged.

"She also ate part of our last suspects." Alyssa chimed in.

"Spines are not tasty." The attempted joke fell short of any reaction.

Karina looked bewildered. "Wouldn't she have been infected?"

"Oh, yes. But that doesn't make her a monster, anymore than being a Rusalka does." Alyssa grinned.

Karina lifted the cake to her nose. "Why would you eat this?" She asked. "It smells weird."

Alyssa sighed. "We should get going."

Granddad and Grandma laughed.

Karina looked uncomfortably between the two of us. "I'm going to need you to explain how you can be infected by that and-"

"You're safe, Karina." I said, quietly. "I promise."

Karina nodded. "All the same, I'll take a Taxi back."

A long time ago

April 17th, 2009

Afghanistan

Zilla

I grumbled as I dusted myself off for the third time this hour. The sandstorm bit at my lungs, and my lungs wanted to hiss at it.

Of course, I couldn't do that. I couldn't scream Rusalkan epithets about this stupid damn desert. People didn't understand Rusalkan but they understood enough *other* languages to understand what Rusalkan *wasn't.*

I hated this place. I had been stuck here for a while. Ever since my grievance leave expired.

We were guarding a medical convoy. That was our job. Most of the Canadian forces deployed here were peacekeeping forces, at this point. Generally, that was our job, anyway. The Americans bomb the crap out of everything, we bring medical convoys through and then they rebuild the middle east only for the Americans to bomb the crap out of it again in about a decade. Vicious circle.

The wind blew my hair into my face. I groaned. My rifle probably needed cleaning. *Again.* So did the rest of me.

The convoy came across a crumbling house. The team doing metal detection to prevent IEDs from destroying our convoy was starting to look weary. We had to walk, after all. I held up my hand in a closed fist.

The vehicles all stopped in order.

"Fan out, then set up camp." I presumed my instructions were clear. This was usually incorrect.

"Captain, with due respect, we've got a long way still to go." One of the other officers retorted.

"Did that sound like a suggestion that was open for debate, Petty Officer?" My tone turned stern and authoritative.

"Harm's got a point. There's cover here. We might even be able to start a fire in the windscreen this building is providing." A stern voice retorted. Doctor Vanille had almost as commanding a tone as I did, and as he gave those of us on foot a look over, he nodded. I hated that people listened to him over me. I couldn't show it. We had to be *civil* to each other. Unfortunately. "Weather like this can kill us if we're not careful. It's easy for you to say this isn't a good place to rest, Petty Officer. You're driving the car. You're also a Petty Officer. We follow the Captain's orders. Not your own impatience."

"That's generally how a military hierarchy works." Sarcasm had a tendency to break through to people. As did shouting. They were the only methods I could think of to assert control of the situation again that didn't involve violence. "It's *Captain Williams*, Doctor Vanille, and I SAID FAN OUT. Sweep this location and make sure it's safe."

The team hastily evacuated the vehicles in the convoy, and began searching the surrounding areas for signs of anything possibly dangerous.

I turned on my rifle light, and began checking the rubble of the damaged building.

There was a quiet noise of someone struggling to move against rocks. Not something humans could easily hear. I hastily moved towards it, weapon out.

A young woman, perhaps 13 or 14, was sitting in a corner, quietly whimpering. There were rocks covering one of her legs.

My flashlight scanned the area around the room, and my nostrils flared, tasting the harsh air.

My nose caught the scent of the blood before my flashlight did.

Blood stained bricks covered the caved in part of the room.

"Hal 'ant wahadk?" I asked, though my Russian-esque/Canadian hybrid accent did interfere with how clearly my arabic might be understood.

"English. Yes." The girl said, quietly. "They." She pointed at the rubble. "Gone."

I lowered my rifle. "I need a medic in here!" I shouted, before kneeling next to the girl. "What's your name?" I asked, quietly.

"Zilla." The girl said, quietly.

"Is this where your family lived?" I looked around what was left of the building. There was a blanket and an empty water bottle. No food was in sight and the room was otherwise fairly bare.

"They gone now." Zilla said quietly. She pointed up. "They went home."

It took a few minutes to follow what that meant, before I nodded and gently started removing the rubble from around her.

Doctor Vanille frowned as they entered, and observed the scene. "Is she alive?"

"Yes, and that's my concern. She has no supplies left, but doesn't appear unhealthy. You look after her. This might be a trap." I nodded. "And if it's not a trap, this damage was recent. Either the Americans did this or the bad guys of the week did, and I'd rather not find out which."

"Yes, Captain." Vanille nodded. He never was one to like it when I shouted at him.

The girl shook her head. "DO NOT-!"

Vanille frowned, and took a step back. "I'm not going to hurt you."

"That's not it." I shook my head. "You're not familiar, and you're a man. That's my mistake. I'll do some basic first aid. You get the others to set up defensively."

Vanille nodded and handed me the first aid kit, before rushing out.

"I am Captain Williams." I told the girl while taking a seat next to her on the floor, and offered her my canteen. "But you can just call me Harmony, okay?"

The girl nodded and laid her head against my shoulder, not taking the offered water.

She closed her eyes.

Somewhere in the back of my mind, instincts stirred. For he first time since Lauren died, I smiled as I wrapped an arm around her.

"You're safe, Zilla. I promise."

The young woman took that as permission to fall asleep.

That was a good mission statement. A good code to live by.

I will keep you safe.

For the first time in a couple years my heart found purpose again and as I sat there, cradling the orphaned child, I knew exactly what I had to do next.

Save the girl.

Day 1

March 14th, 2020

A miraculous end

The base was quiet when we pulled on. The air was crisp and the grounds had the traditional spring problem of too many dandelions. The air stunk of them, not that humans much noticed their scent. It was less a scent than a pheremonal discharge, really, and humans were much less understanding of such scents.

It certainly wasn't my favorite smell in the world. Then again, that probably was not a hard thing for one to guess upon learning that my species was not especially native to places they grew.

It wasn't entirely fair to the plant to judge it by the nose of an aquatic predator when one considered the smells I WAS fond of were routinely considered *vile* by humans. There had been a massive beaching of anchovies, for example, and while they certainly were a pleasant smell to seagulls and myself, most people had been grateful the seagulls ate most of them, so as to limit what humans referred to as a *stench*.

Alyssa had stopped joining me on my runs along the beach for exactly that scent, and had been grateful, once it passed.

Now, she smiled at the yellow spotted lawns as we drove up to the CFCIS building, and I shook my head. "They *are* weeds, you know?"

"What is a flower, if not a weed who has become beautiful enough to be treated kindly?" Alyssa retorted.

I was well aware that the saying applied to more than just the yellow flora as we exited the car. It was as much a commentary on myself, as the flowers and suitably chastised by decidedly romantic poetry, I held up my ID to the building guards and we entered in silence.

As we stepped into the collective office of my team, I nodded to the familiar faces of Jill Zaheer, who looked particularly troubled, as she had for most of this calendar year, and Vincent Lasenza, who was a very difficult man to force into a concerned mood.

Neither one of us had to ask why Jill was apprehensive. Her once home was on the brink of war for the Posiedon-knows-how-many-eth time, since she had been born. It always left her in an understandably foul state.

Having served there, myself, I knew it imprudent to discuss the topic. It still made me a bit nostalgic for the first time I had met the girl and I found myself reminded of her by every simple thing, from the promise I had made to Karina, to my sudden craving to comfort her. Without a word, I wrapped her in a hug and gently rubbed her back in the same manner that I had during our time in that peace forsaken desert.

It also filled me with a reminder that this young woman was the embodiment of why I had stopped being an *officer of the armed forces* and had instead become a *military police officer*.

Jill looked up quietly, and offered a silent nod of appreciation. "You shouldn't have come."

"Why not?" Vinny asked in what was his typical ignorance of the surrounding atmospheric attitude. "If we've got a case, we need Harm."

Jill shook her head. "It is her day of mourning, idiot. We have this discussion every year."

Vinny looked perplexed.

"Lauren would be 14." Jill filled in the blanks.

Vinny's eyes widened and he nodded, looking away.

The elevator dinged and Jill and Vinny's attention were drawn to the soft noise of the wheelchair as it ticked along the poorly maintained tile floor.

"Ladies. Gentlemen. May I introduce Leftenant Karina Gill of Military Intelligence. I presume you understand why she's here." Alyssa gestured. "This is Chief Petty Officer Jill Zaheer, and Chief Petty Officer Vincent Lasenza."

"A pleasure." Vinny held out his hand.

"So I've heard." Karina noted, nodding to Jill, but not shaking either hand. "I'm told you are all read in on the classified information surrounding Commander Williams."

"Yup." Vinny nodded.

"I'm not sure we're read in on all of it. Harmony seems to think there's more that neither she, nor we are being informed of." Jill retorted.

Karina gestured to Jill and Alyssa. "So you two really are the clever ones, then."

"Hey!" Vinny and I said in approximate unison.

"Yes." Jill and Alyssa's response was nearly matched in its uniformity.

Karina gave an amused smirk, before nodding. "Officially, this case is not being investigated by the Canadian Forces Criminal Investigative Service."

"Which implies that the circumstances of this case do not warrant a standard criminal investigation." Alyssa filled in.

"Very good." Karina nodded. "I'm told you were briefed on the case already."

Vinny looked blank.

"Car accident. Leftenant Jeremy Franks and his mother, Wendy Franks." Jill said, digging through her messy desk, until she withdrew the black file. "I've been doing some digging between cases."

"As have I." A thickly accented voice said from behind Karina, as Doctor Zehlendorf stepped around the woman. "Greetings, Leftenant. I was warned of your arrival and took the time to tidy up so the good Chief Petty Officers and their proclivity for leaving this place a disastrous mess would not impede your navigation."

"When were you informed of that?" Karina asked.

"When Leftenant Sanchez texted me, as they left the Commander's home." Zehlendorf said, matter-of-factly. "Wendy Franks was a particularly peculiar autopsy." The man paused to collect his thoughts, before picking up copies of the autopsy report and handing them out. "The city M.E. did not understand why I wanted the bodies, let alone to perform an autopsy on them, but fortunately CFNIS has default jurisdiction on Navy personnel dying of even obvious causes that shouldn't require one. Wendy Franks had not a single trace of cancer in her body. That was the peculiar part. Lung cancer leaves behind traces. Lungs are terrible at healing scars from bacterial infections, cancers, and viruses. This woman's lungs were as pristine as a newborn child."

I winced at the comment, though Zehlendorf did not notice.

"In point of fact, the woman was uncannily healthy for her age. Her bones showed no signs of the wear and tear of being 50. She had no traces of ever having fought off anything, ever. Her blood chemistry was abnormally perfect for a healthy 20 year old. If I was not informed of the peculiar nature of our future cases, I would be extremely curious about every single step of this woman's autopsy, because it was *impossibly* clean and to the point." He finished.

"Which is where my interest was piqued." Karina nodded. "People just don't miraculously recover from stage 4 lung cancer and then die in a car crash two weeks later."

"What about the Leftenant?" Jill asked.

"That's where it gets interesting." Zehlendorf nodded. "He, unlike his mother, showed every single sign of his military career in his autopsy, right down to the run-in with a nasty pneumonia infection while at sea. Everything about this young man was expected, barring one single detail."

There was a moment of silence that prodded the doctor on.

"There was no explanation for why a sober and healthy young man with good eyesight ended up at fault in a perfectly preventable car crash, in a vehicle which was mechanically sound at the time of the crash." Karina filled in.

Jill's eyebrow raised.

"Maybe he just drove like Guppy does." Alyssa suggested.

There was a hearty chuckle shared by all but Karina, who shook her head.

Karina extended a USB drive to Jill. "Surveillance footage of the crash. He was stopped at the red light. Waited for traffic to start crossing in front of him, and then, as though he could not see said traffic and assumed the light had turned green, he began a normal, slow acceleration, and was promptly smashed up pretty bad by a garbage truck. All on camera."

Now, she had Jill's fascination piqued, and both mine, and Alyssa's, as well, though Vinny looked dismissive. "This isn't our case." He noted, dryly.

"This would not be our case, were there not a black file on the topic." Jill corrected.

"Very good, Miss Zaheer. I'm going to like having an intellectual equal on hand. It's remarkably uncommon in the intelligence department." Karina dug into her bag, and withdrew two new black files. "These two are new. They happened yesterday, and this morning. A chief warrant officer was set to be discharged for injuries in combat, and woke up miraculously healed. An air force pilot who lost her ability to see during a crash was miraculously rendered capable of perfect eyesight. These cases would be enough to grab our interest, but what's more fascinating is that they both perished exactly two weeks after their miracles in obscure, and improbable ways. Chief Warrant Officer Jefferies drowned while emptying the dishwasher while home on leave, and Captain Briant wasn't watching where she was going, slipped on a banana peel, and was impaled upon a decorative plant."

"Accidents happen, new girl." Vince rolled his eyes.

"Karina, or Leftenant Gill." Karina corrected. "And you're being deliberately obtuse."

"No, no." I shook my head. "We've been over this. That's his natural setting. He doesn't actively work at it."

Vince gave me a look of utter betrayal at this comment.

"How in the absolute heck does one drown in a dishwasher?" Zehlendorf asked.

Vince blinked, then his eyes went wide. "Oh."

Karina shook her head before handing the doctor the two files. "The bodies are being transported here today. I'm hoping you can tell me, because if it's *not* beyond the realm of the explainable, then this isn't our case and we can spend the evening having a quiet meal, in sheer peace and tranquility."

"You just had to curse it." Vince winced.

"I did no such thing. I don't even have a hex bag on me." Karina gave him a frown.

"Not literally. Vince is superstitious. By wishing for a calm and peaceful day, you're pretty much guaranteeing that we won't have one in his eyes." Jill filled in. "Can you make hex bags?"

"Officially, no, I have no occult knowledge, cannot practice 23 separate variations of what you would consider witchcraft, and definitely do not speak either Latin, nor a peculiar Ukranian dialect exclusive to siren folk." Karina shrugged.

"And unofficially?" Vince asked.

"Unofficially, you're an idiot." Karina retorted. "That was a very specific list of things that I cannot do, for which you would have no real reason to expect that I would."

"Which is why I asked *what you could do*." Vince prompted.

Karina hissed a word in Rusalkan which meant *Idiot man-child*, and Vince did not grasp that he was being insulted.

I gave her an amused nod. It was almost a pleasant thing to hear someone else speak that language. Were it not for recent events, it would probably feel even more pleasant, though those who spoke Rusalkan were not particularly high on my comfort zone list after the vampiric plague incident.

"She's not going to tell you, Vince. It's classified." Alyssa said, helpfully.

"Ah. Secret agent lady. Super secret and very clandestine. Does your wheelchair have a hidden minigun, or something?" Vince asked.

Karina gave him a perplexed look. "No. It just- I- It's a perfectly normal- WHY WOULD YOU ASK THAT?"

"He watches WAYYYYY too many spy thriller movies." Jill filled in.

Karina closed her eyes. "Posiedon protect us all." She whispered below what would normally be audible to human ears. "Regardless of THAT unnecessary exploration into the depths of the Petty Officer's idiocy, this is a black file case specifically because of the incidents prior to the deaths being *unnaturally fortuitous*, and then terrible things happening after the precise amount of time as each other event has passed. That implies a curse, or price required to be paid within a specific timeframe."

"Look, I got lucky on the horse races two weeks ago, but I ain't in the hospital." Vince shrugged.

"How lucky?" Jill frowned. "If it was big, you'd be shoving it in our faces."

"Unless it was really big, because *somebody* has been talking non-stop about how much she wants new ear pods and is mad she can't afford them." Alyssa chimed in.

Vince nodded. "And she still owes me $300 bucks for that pair of shoes she ruined."

"How big?" Karina asked.

Vince shook his head. "I ain't talkin', secret agent lady."

"Fifty seven thousand." I filled in, helpfully. "On a pony that had no place winning that race."

Vince winced.

"How do you know?" Jill asked.

"She was there. Harm insists upon making sure I don't go to the race track alone, after… incidents." Vince replied. "Never thought she'd rat me out, though."

"Well, that certainly sounds like a big win." Karina nodded. "You're lucky you didn't get into trouble for that. Some bookkeepers aren't exactly nice people about unexpected windfalls."

"That part wasn't luck. That was Harm."

A less long time ago

August 31st, 2012

Hastings Racecourse, Vancouver

Vincent

It was a particularly warm and sunny afternoon. Prime race day weather. I leaned against one of the viewing box walls, patiently, with my earpiece uncomfortably making my ears sweat against the terrible rubber feeling.

It was air conditioned in here, certainly, but we were also planning a takedown of a very big underground book keeper and this was not the kind of situation one wanted to be in on an overcrowded Saturday afternoon, in an incredibly public place with tens of thousands of people unaware they could be turned into collateral damage or hostages.

This entire case revolved around one army idiot who had gotten in deep, and whose safety had been threatened while on base.

Chief Warrant Officer Vincent Lasenza was an irritating, yet vaguely charming army man who had previously worked in an armory in the middle east, prior to his leave, here in Vancouver. He seemed like a nice enough guy, in spite of more than a few jilted lovers(not that I was in a position to criticize) which is why the entire incident had caught me by surprise when it had been reported.

Now, as I watched him sweating as his stupid horse came in 5th, I found myself increasingly worried both for him, and those around him.

"That's more money you owe me, Lasenza." Came a grumpy voice from the microphone he was wearing. "You had better pay up today, or we'll be having words about this. I've had enough waiting."

Of course, unbeknownst to this would-be mob boss, this was the entire point. Running an unlicensed gambling ring was a crime in most non-reservation places above the Mexican border in North America, and this man definitely did not work for the British Columbia Lottery Corporation. Of course, running an illegal gambling ring wasn't a big enough crime to warrant most agencies caring about it, outside the Gambling Enforcement agency, and it was they who had put this sting operation together. The only reason I was allowed to be in on it was because the case involved military personnel.

The next move was critical.

Vince stood very still before dashing frantically towards the exits.

The man gave an almost smile before following him at a casual pace.

I followed him as casually as possible, staying well out of sight.

"Target is leaving." I said, quietly. "Like a proper bloodhound following the scent."

"Lasenza is probably glad he's not on this channel. I doubt he'd appreciate that wording." Came the soft voice of gambling enforcement officer Lyra Bell. She irritated me in a less charming way and something about her set off my instincts in an *uncomfortable* way.

Of course, *in an uncomfortable way* wasn't definitive proof of anything, but just to be sure, I had confirmed our op existed with the Gambling Enforcement agency.

As the parking lot loomed in front of me I quickly lost sight of the man in question and my attention was drawn back from my instincts to the chase. Vincent's life was in my hands. This book keeper wasn't known to be kind to people who tried running from gambling debts and Vincent's deployment date was deliberately leaked to him as being within the week.

"Well, I'll give you this much credit." A thick Italian accent said, from behind me. "You're certainly relentless."

I turned around, and drew my weapon.

It was kicked out of my hand.

The balding book keeper clapped his hands. "You really thought you could come into my city and treat me like a common criminal?"

I looked between him and whoever had kicked my gun out of my hand.

Both this man and the familiar face of Lyra Bell had guns drawn on me.

"As far as the gambling Enforcement agency is concerned?" Lyra asked. "This tip was not credible and this op never happened. You went rogue, tried to do it anyway out of some poorly thought out campaign for justice."

"I should have known." I groaned. "There's no way someone could operate an elaborate betting ring at this track without someone on the inside."

The book keeper laughed heartily.

Right before Vince snuck up behind him, and sucker punched him to the ground.

Bell turned, surprised, and that was all I needed. Just that brief distraction.

My knee came up and my arm came down. Her gun arm was in-between. There was a satisfying *snap* as at least one of the bones in her arm was broken, and she screamed, dropping the gun.

Several armed people arrived shortly thereafter, weapons drawn. "Gambling Enforcement. DO NOT MOVE!"

"What?" Bell asked, through gritted teeth.

"Guess you're just lucky your informant was incredibly suspicious, and called your boss to confirm an op he knew nothing about." One of the other officers said, shrugging.

"That part wasn't luck." Vince said, gesturing between the two. "Luck was me getting the drop on the big guy. The rest of it? That was just Harm. She's got a reputation."

I shrugged. "What can I say? Dad always said to measure twice and cut once, whenever you were trying to build something."

"Or break someone's arm." Vince added.

"Oh, no. Mom taught me how to do that when I was in seventh grade and Big John was bullying me for my accent."

Day 1

(Again)

Poor unfortunate corpses

Lunch was a quiet adventure as Alyssa and I impatiently waited for the autopsy results. Giving up on what passed for our ability to wait, we both made our way into the morgue, surprised to discover that Karina had beaten us there.

Zehlendorf nodded to us both. "Commander. Leftenant." He said, calmly. "I'm afraid these two are just as perplexing as the others, in that their bodies show no unhealthy signs of anything beyond their cause of death."

"Nothing." Karina added. "No symbols. No insignias. If they were branded by whatever cursed them to such an unfortunate end, it wasn't on their physical bodies."

"You were expecting to find something?" Alyssa asked.

"Well, naturally. Most creatures that take sacrifices in exchange for magic like this brand their victims in some way." Karina held up a heart in her hands, looking at it curiously. "Nothing. Not a scratch, or strained muscle, and this woman performed combat maneuvers in an outdated helicopter in Afghanistan."

"Very bewildering indeed." Zehlendorf agreed. "There is supposed to be scarring here-" Zehlendorf pointed. "-and here, from shrapnel wounds, but there is nothing."

"It's like something gave her a brand new body, and then when she couldn't pay for it, they took it away." Karina tilted the heart. "Nothing was missing from the body, either, that wasn't impaled on the plant."

"Also, she was wearing practically new hiking boots." Zehlendorf added.

"Yes. And that's relevant because?" I gave them both a confused look.

"Hiking boots are generally designed to prevent slipping, even on slippery terrain like ice. The odds of slipping on a banana peel outside of a cartoon or video game are… low." Alyssa filled in.

"Computer simulations just don't say it's supposed to happen." Karina tilted her head to a report next to her. "Jill says it's as probable as drowning in a dishwasher."

"Why are you getting my team's reports before I am?" I asked in a particularly serious tone that implied the answer had better be **good**.

Zehlendorf shifted uncomfortably. "I told her you weren't going to like that, but–"

"Due respect, ma'am, this is a time sensitive thing if I'm right, and I just didn't have the time for you to finish your romantic lunch date." Karina didn't even bother looking at me.

"Well, I do hope your affairs are in order." Zehlendorf noted. "I'll prepare your drawer. Calling it now. Time of death, 1337, Pacific daylight."

"Quiet." I said, pointing a finger at him. "No. We've been sitting there. Waiting. For a text. For a call. For anything. And because they're giving the reports to you, presuming you'll fill me in, we're wasting our time. It was not romantic. Alyssa was doing an impromptu psych assessment of the crime scenes, and I was trying to keep myself sane by reading background information, while *nobody told us anything*, so let me make this PERFECTLY clear, *Leftenant.* I am the Commanding Officer of this team. I may not expect my team to respect me as a person, or to treat many of my personality quirks with any degree of kindness, but when it comes to who is in charge, I do not tolerate anyone presuming it isn't me. I don't watch over Jill, nor Doctor Zehlendorf's shoulders because I trust them to *do their jobs* so that I may do mine. By interfering with the chain of command, and presuming that I am uncaring, or unavailable, you are interfering with both their and my ability to do so, *and I will not tolerate that.* You can talk shit about me showing overt favoritism to Alyssa. You can insult Vinny's intelligence, or complain about Jill's functional mess of a workstation. You can make all the comments you want about the weird kite collection Doctor Zehlendorf has in his office, and you can do whatever bizarre quirk it is you do to increase your own productivity and I won't give a Posiedon damned crap." I took a moment to dramatically hold up just one finger between us. "If you ever try to commandeer my team, or my investigation again, I will write you up for insubordination so fast your head will spin. You are assigned *to* my team. My team is not assigned *to you.* I suggest you learn that distinction very, VERY fast."

Karina looked bewildered at this, and held up her hands in surrender. "Look, I'm sorry, I just thought you were busy, and-"

"Don't. Don't explain it. Don't dig yourself any further. Do not say another damn word that is not *yes* and *ma'am,* in that exact order. Am I clear?" I asked.

Karina inclined her head. "Yes, ma'am."

"Good. Get out and grab yourself something to drink. I need to have a word about operational procedure with Doctor Zehlendorf, then Miss Zaheer." I said, calming down.

Karina hastily wheeled herself out of the morgue after washing her hands.

"Wow. You do know how much-" Alyssa began.

I held up the same finger towards her.

"-this isn't the time or place for this discussion." She finished, hastily leaving.

"You should have called me." I told the Doctor, irritated. "After everything, you, of all people? Jill, I understand. She's outranked."

Zehlendorf sighed. "Just like Beirut, is it not?"

"I hope not. If she's gunning for my job and you're helping her, I'm going to be *very* cross, Alfred." I narrowed my eyes. "Last time, it didn't end well."

"Last time, she ended up on one of these slabs after an overconfident attempt to take down an insurgent group on her own." Zehlendorf nodded. "Of course, it wasn't *this* her."

"And you helped *that* her do it." I crossed my arms.

"Listen, I didn't think any harm would come. She just wanted to sit in on the autopsy. When I realized Jill brought her that report, I told her you weren't going to like her pulling this stunt, but she didn't care." Zehlendorf held up both viscera covered hands. "I'm not trying anything, and there are no ulterior motives, but I do have to do this autopsy, and I could not particularly lock her out, given that she also outranks *me* after that incident with the man in the place."

I took a breath, and nodded. "Sorry." I evened out my tone.

"What was that?" Zehlendorf grinned brightly. "That could not have been what I thought it was."

"I'm sorry." I squared my shoulders, and gave him a glare. "I just wasn't expecting someone to so casually try and usurp my job, and I got defensive. I never should have doubted your intentions. Especially after Iraq."

Zehlendorf grinned. "Now *that* was an adventure."

"Not half as much of an adventure as that time someone tried vamprizing the Greater Vancouver Regional District." I retorted.

"This is why I would never intentionally betray you, Commander. You and I have entirely too much fun together. I'd sooner give up my kites, than cause you any harm." Zehlendorf nodded.

"Your *kites*?" I gave him a mocking glare. "I thought for sure I'd rate at least higher than your kids."

"Those little shits who can't even remember my birthday?" Zehlendorf asked, fake-outraged. "You think they rate above my *kites*?"

"Okay, point." I held up my hands. "I've got to go restore my authority with-"

Jill stepped into the morgue with an unpleasant look on her face. "Leftenant Sanchez said you wanted to see me, ma'am?"

"She already knows she's in große Scheiße." Zehlendorf chuckled.

"Harmony, I swear-" Jill began.

I held up my hands, and shook my head. "Alfred already reminded me that you were just doing your job."

Jill gave the doctor a relieved look.

"In the future, *Zilla*." I added.

"I'll come to you first, even if the Prime Minister of Canada needs the results, ma'am." Jill nodded.

"I was GOING TO SAY that you and I have gone through enough shit that you don't have to address me as ma'am, but I quite like your response better. What have you got for me?" I gave her a very bemused look to reassure her.

"Computer simulations. Crime scene sketches. Witness accounts. Surveillance footage. Blood chemistry panels. They all say the same thing, Harmony."

"That not a single one of these people has any logical reasoning for being dead?"

"Exactly."

The fourth

The alarms rang throughout the base and every single person around us had snapped to full attention. "This is not a drill. All stations, repeat, this is not a drill."

I drew my firearm as I began searching the building for anything unexpected when I was approached by Captain Salisbury. "Commander, please follow me."

"What happened?" I asked, hastily falling into a triple time march behind the base commander.

"There was an explosion in the armory. Chief Petty Officer Lasenza." Salisbury paused. "He is not well."

I stopped my march and stared at the man, blankly.

"What do you mean by-" I paused to make air quotes. "-he's not well?" I asked.

"It appears that while he was cleaning the armed response kits in the armory, something caused an explosion. If it were not for Leftenant Gill being on her way to find him and performing some rushed first aid, the doctors do not think he would be okay." Salisbury said. "Come, come. She said she had something important to discuss with you."

"Like how she's withholding shit from me and how she knew he was in danger." I grumbled under my breath, as I resumed my pace.

We went past the armory and something caught my attention. Smells. Something obviously not right.

Chlorine gas. Ammonia.

That didn't sit well with me, but I kept going. Vince might have been an idiot, sure, but he had also been an armory officer and *explosives expert* for a decade. It seemed like a rookie mistake to use cleaning products that had a known explosive interaction together.

It seemed almost like-

-well, almost like a comically stupid mistake.

My brain jogged to catch up to this thought.

Look, I got lucky on the horse races two weeks ago, but I ain't in the hospital.

Vinny's words almost seemed to be taunting, now.

We approached the medical bay, and my entire body lurched. *Blood. Burnt meat.* Smells that would have turned my stomach, were I human.

It took a moment to regain control of my body. My blood was pumping too fast. The lights were too loud. The other smells became stronger. Deodorants. Disinfectants. One of the nurses had had some Thai food for lunch.

It used to be that this was less overwhelming. I used to have better control of my instinctive responses.

That was before the stupid virus. Now I had to restrain myself from baring my less human teeth as my body tried to take instinctive control. Like the virus had installed a second version of Harmony. Somehow more hedonistic. Angry.

I had to clench my fists to hide the slight webbing forming, and the sharpened claws extending. I closed my eyes, and focused on the only things that kept me going. The Job. The promise. Alyssa.

Salisbury, entirely unaware of this struggle, gestured at the surgery ward. "I'll leave you to your friend."

I appreciated this newfound respect that the Commanding Officer of the base offered and I took a deep breath, relieved to be left alone for a moment.

It was short lived as a familiar scent intruded upon the room. I gave the newest member of my team a glare for the intrusion.

"What happened?" I asked through siren teeth and in a particularly hissing tone.

Karina gave me an uncomfortable look and she shifted in her seat. "Something that shouldn't have happened. A chemical reaction between cleaning solvents caused an explosion. The armory isn't a great place for that. I'd say we're lucky only one person was issued-"

"Except it shouldn't have happened at all." I nodded.

"There is... Something." Karina said, quietly. "He stopped rapidly declining when I put together an antimagic field." Karina gestured towards the surgery. "He's making it through. They didn't think he was going to. I think it's a curse."

"An *antimagic* field?" I gave her a perplexed look.

"Does what it says on the tin." Karina nodded. "It's an old spell used to protect people from magical creatures. Mirror, though it can be done with clear glass. Goat's blood. Some Sanskrit. It mutes most commonplace magic, barring a few demonic and godly magics. It was invented by what would be Muslim clerics in today's understanding, to protect people against Jinn." She shrugged. "I might be an entirely inept *sea*witch, but I'm not bad at a LOT of human witchcraft."

"I read about this." Recognition dawned and I turned my attention fully to her, glad to have a distraction. "In the file about Lieutenant Noir. Magical muting."

Karina held up a hand. "I'm the one who uncovered the spell to do that, but I didn't intend for it to be misused as it was. It had been lost in I-can't-tell-you-istan for centuries." She nodded to Vince. "I'll get started on a tea that should help purge the curse from him, but Commander?" She gave a frown to the surgery ward. "There aren't many beings who pull this sort of thing. If this antimagic field is working, it's not a demon. I'm worried that my original suspicion was correct."

"That this is seawitch magic." I nodded. "Or something close enough for government work."

"You can call it close enough. I have to figure out what is doing this, so I can stop them." Karina scowled. "If this isn't a seawitch curse, the tea is just going to be some really bitter tea with some pretty disgusting ingredients that he will *not* thank me for making him drink."

I slowly began to relax and my sharper teeth receded. "Thank you, Karina."

She shook her head. "The pack protects itself, or it dies. You don't owe me any thanks."

"You're saving Vince's life. That's worthy of praise in my book." I placed a hand on her shoulder. "And that's enough for me to trust you at face value. I'm sorry I exploded earlier."

Karina visibly relaxed at that. "Grab your gear, then. We've got work to do."

"We always do."

A while ago

2014

Beirut, Lebanon

Alfred and Victor

The ocean air filled my lungs for the first time in months, and my entire body vibrated with excitement.

I wish I could have said this was a good time to enjoy the ocean, but unfortunately, we had been lost in Syria trying to chase down a group of people who had kidnapped two of our idiot *peacemakers*.

Doctor Quinn Burnette had taken it upon herself to try and take down a militant group that had been raiding medical convoys. She had done so alongside another doctor. The two were incensed over the fact that the military refused to authorize a mission into Syria to track them down.

Alongside Doctor Victor Vanille, she had stolen gear from our American counterparts, *borrowed* a vehicle, and went after them thinking there were Bitch and Dumbass, or something.

It wasn't unclear as to her motives. I had recommended against the mission, and she had been systematically attempting to undermine *the great Captain Williams*(as others liked to put it).

Recovering them was my last official mission attached to the Army's Peace Corps.

Unfortunately, it was a sad ending.

Doctor Zehlendorf stood next to me, as we looked at the caskets.

"Idiots." Zehlendorf said, quietly. "I'm sorry."

I'm sorry was hardly something I needed to hear. I had given up on Victor Vanille not long after our recovery of Zilla. His only relation to me as an Ex-husband was an empty one. The love left that marriage when our daughter had died. Working with him had only made it evaporate faster because I began to understand how *catastrophically stupid* the man could be.

And now we stood, the only honor guard over tweedle dee and tweedle dumb, and Alfred looked as exasperated as I felt.

These two had been a gigantic pain in both of our asses ever since the Taliban had attempted to take the base we were stationed and they decided the Army's response wasn't appropriate.

"They were doctors." I said, quietly.

"She was practically a child." Alfred added. "About the age you were, when I first met you."

"That's a long time ago." I said, thoughtfully.

"Very." Alfred agreed. "He never did come back, did he?"

I shook my head. "No. When I was lost, I found Zilla. My brain found a new purpose. She pulled me back. He always... retained that lost purpose recklessness. He kept desperately searching for something to give him meaning, but it never made up for Lauren. She haunted him and he ran from that until the day he died."

"A cruel fate." Alfred said, quietly.

"And one she abused." I agreed. "I'll be glad to be closer to home. I'm tired of this desert. I missed Zilla graduating from her forensics classes."

Alfred smiled at that. "I miss that delightful lasagna your grandmother made."

"That, too." I admitted.

We looked up, grateful to see a group of allied soldiers walking towards us.

"It's time to go home." Alfred said, quietly.

"Grab your gear, then. We've got work to do." I nodded, as the honor guard collected the caskets.

"We always do." Alfred said, quietly. "That's the nature of our jobs, I suppose."

"Still can't believe you're giving up medicine to become a medical examiner."

"Listen, you try getting shot in the buttocks, while trying to perform CPR on someone during a combat situation. I'm looking forward to patients that don't try and stab me, as well."

"Unless they're a zombie."

"Or a vampire."

Day 2

March 15th, 2020

(Richmond Naval Base, Richmond, British Columbia, Canada)

Spear fishing

The armory still smelt of burnt flesh, chemicals, and smoke. My eyes watered at the stench of it as we waded into what was now our crime scene, after the fire department and Hazmat teams had cleared it.

Jill was already hard at work. She looked like she had been crying for hours.

"He's stable." I said, quietly. "For the moment. Doctors are keeping him sedated."

There was a pause in Jill's movements and she took a deep breath. Jill wasn't the most obvious of people, but that small moment was a wash of relief that she needed.

"Alright." Karina clapped her hands. "Where did the blast originate and have you used any sulfuric, or cleaning compounds near there? Are you wearing anything that's scented with sage or lavender? Has anyone used any salt based chemicals in this room?"

Jill looked bewildered for a moment.

"Assume they're pertinent questions." I added.

"Strange questions." Alyssa said, from what had once been Vince's workstation. "This was the initial point of explosion, but it doesn't make any sense."

"As it shouldn't." Karina nodded. "If I'm right, anyway."

"No salt. No cleaning agents. None of that. Potassium Bicarbonate from the fire extinguisher." Jill said, quietly. "Why?"

"Salt, some cleaning agents, and some plants like sage and lavender interfere with witchcraft." Karina said, digging through her bag, before withdrawing a small black pot. She placed it in front of Alyssa, at the blast point. "Hey, do you have any iron in your kit?"

"No." Jill shook her head. "Iron isn't commonly used anymore."

"Drat." Karina said, before digging through her bag again. "I was going to try and make some magic resistant bullets." She added, idly. "Anyway." She pulled out a black vial and a purple vial. "Attunement potion. Tunes itself to the last magical event in the area." She poured it into the pot. "And a tracking spell." She added, tipping the black one in.

There was a loud bubbling, and then something angry and green lashed out of the pot, smacked Karina out of her wheelchair, and then dissolved into a fluid that ate through the pot, table, and the floor under the table.

"Not. Good." Karina groaned, as she sat her wheelchair upright. "Not good at all."

"What the HELL was that?" Alyssa demanded.

"That was the protection spell surrounding the person who cursed Chief Petty Officer Lasenza being forced to reveal its nature by the tracking spell, while deflecting the tracking spell." Karina awkwardly climbed into her chair. "I got it. Don't anyone help, or anything."

"Was that… a tentacle?" I asked.

Karina nodded. "Diagnostic. The spell was cecaelian in origin."

"That's Seawitch." I clarified. "We still don't know how to track whoever did this down."

"This is insane." Jill added. "A Seawitch is murdering people."

"It's lore appropriate." Karina corrected, looking down the hole created by her potion. "Wow. That's deep. Anyway, traditionally, a Seawitch sets a specific time period to achieve a specific goal. They also tend to take a price in exchange. If you can't pay, or can't achieve the goal-"

"You end up in intensive care. Or the morgue." Alyssa finished.

"So, they're like super evil fairy godmothers?" Jill asked.

"No, no. Super evil fairy godmothers are called *crossroads demons*. Seawitches are much more chaotic neutral. They're not out to hurt anyone. They want something. Someone else wants something. It's pure capitalism. They expect to be paid for their magic." Karina explained. "Though there *are* fairy godmothers people construe as dark, or evil."

"Having met one, I consider that opinion overrated." I retorted. "Black Fae are as good, or evil, as you, or I."

"As are Seawitches." Karina agreed. "They're just more selfish, generally. And I don't recall specifying *which* Fae are dark, or evil. There are several thousand iterations of Fae lore, of which I have files that state several hundred of them are confirmed to exist."

"I'm really not sure I like this." Jill protested.

"You think you got it bad?" Karina asked. "I'm the one who has to formulate the dispelling charm that keeps Vince alive, and then we have to find, and kill one of my-"

She froze.

"One of your what?" Jill asked.

"Nevermind." Karina said, quietly. "Forget I said anything."

"Jill doesn't forget things very often." Alyssa laughed. "Good luck with that."

Jill shook her head. "Don't worry about whatever it was. I'm too busy to care, anyway."

I knelt down next to Jill, and placed a hand on her back. "We're going to stop this."

Jill laughed. "Magic. We're going to stop a homicidal supernatural squid witch."

Karina tilted her head. "It wouldn't be the first time."

"We helped a fairy godmother stop a homicidal vampire rusalka." I pointed out. I bared my siren teeth. "While I *was* a homicidal vampire rusalka."

Alyssa held up a finger. "Keep in mind, the homicidal vampire rusalka was married to a KGB officer."

Jill leaned her head against my shoulder. "This is personal. Harmony." Jill's voice fell to a whisper. "Whoever did this, they came after our family. They did it in OUR HOME."

I was silenced by this. It hadn't quite hit me exactly how unpleasantly familiar that situation must have been for her, until I heard her say those words.

"Then we hunt them down." Alyssa's tone was that of anger, as though she was just coming to this same conclusion of violation.

"How?" Jill asked. "The magic cauldron tracking spell fizzled."

Karina took a moment, before crossing her arms. "You must not have served."

"We don't give up." I agreed. "We find a new method of tracking."

Jill shook her head. "How? Voodoo?"

"Voodoo? Ink! Never. That's not magic I like to mess with." Karina's shoes fell off, and tentacles stuck out of her pant legs. "We do this the only way we can. We don't hold back, and we do it right."

Jill's gaze looked up at that, and her attention froze on the tentacles.

"Welcome to the secret club." Alyssa nodded. "What do you need?"

"I need as much iron as you can find, and then I'm going to need a chameleon, a frog, a vial of Vince's blood, a can of red bull, and three tuna sandwiches." Karina cleared her throat. "And a new cauldron."

"Alyssa, get the food, I'll get the stuff from the pet shop, Jill, get the blood and something that will do as a cauldron." I tried to sound commanding. "We're going to get this done."

"Something my adopted dad used to teach me." Karina agreed. "Sometimes, you can't fish a sturgeon with a fishing line. Sometimes, you need a spear."

"Well, eye of newt, and tail of italian." Jill took a deep breath. "This is going to be one for the ages."

"Like that time you helped a vampire rusalka kill a vampire rusalka and stop a KGB plan?"

"Our life is so freaking weird."

Fighting fire with a top hat

It took a surprisingly short time to find everything except the cauldron, but how I was going to write up a report that explained to either Captain Salisbury, or PETA, for that matter, why Karina needed live animals was a tough question. The more I thought about it, the more I realized compensating Alyssa out of pocket was probably easier than trying to file an expense report for a Pet-land receipt for a chameleon, and a frog.

Karina gathered the things, and frowned. "Miss Zaheer, you're muslim, correct?"

"Yes." Jill said, quietly. "Why?"

"I have to dissect a chameleon, and remove the eyes of a frog. I'm not sure you really want to be in the room while I-" Karina held up a scalpel.

"Send me a text when you're ready to start with the potion." Jill said, with an uncomfortable nod, before she walked out of the room.

"And the Tuna sandwiches? The Redbull?" Alyssa asked.

Karina pulled some of the tuna out of one of the sandwiches. "Control substance. We eat the tuna sandwiches, and it'll tune us into the spell."

"Why not four?" Alyssa frowned. "What about Jill?"

"Jill is a muslim woman who has an aversion for eating meat, and also she's not a field officer." I pointed out.

"Exactly." Karina agreed. "Now, I should warn you, most of this is… theatrical. Everyone assumes it's like how the sea witch or the Evil Queen does it on TV."

"Theatrical? Why not just cast the spell?" Alyssa gave her an increasingly inquisitive look.

"Jill." I said, simply.

"You must understand." Karina paused to calmly cut into the chameleon. "Jill is at risk. We don't know how people are being targeted. We need to keep up Jill's spirits. If she loses hope and gets desperate to save Vince, she's vulnerable. This isn't just about stopping whoever's doing this. It's about protecting all of us. You have to understand the psyche of who is doing this."

Alyssa looked thoughtful. "Yeah. Okay, that's fair. Vince had a vulnerability. It was abused. If we don't protect each other, and watch our vulnerabilities, we're going to end up-"

"Getting something we want, and if we don't do as we're told, we're dead." I finished.

Karina nodded. "This is as much to save Jill as it is to save Vince."

"You're not half bad, you know?" Alyssa laughed.

"I try. It's… been pointed out that I've been a bit cold towards everyone." Karina paused. "Like Jill said. This was personal. That's important, actually. Which of you two has the closest connection to Vince?"

"That would be the boss lady." Alyssa gestured. "Why?"

"That works nicely." Karina looked relieved. "I was worried it was Jill. I need someone tied to him to tune in to the spell that was cast on him."

"Tune in?" I asked.

"This is not a proper tracking potion." Karina said, before taking some of the chameleon's scales off, and shoving them into the tuna sandwiches. "I don't have magic of my own, but my mother did. That means where my magic WOULD be, there's this... vacant hole? Yeah, the analogy is never going to come close. Anyway, I'm going to use this to our advantage. I'm going to mimic the magic field of whoever cast this very briefly. It'll mean that the protection spell will recognize me as whoever cast the spell, and not prevent me from tracking the spell. The problem would normally be that I can't track a spell I cast, which is why I'm going to trick the tracking spell into thinking YOU are the one who cast it."

"And because you permit it, it'll work." Alyssa blinked. "Won't the tracking spell just lock on you, though?"

"No. That'll use up all the magic I'll be able to borrow. At which point, the tracking spell will lose it's connection to me-" Karina explained.

"-and lock back on whoever cursed Vince." I finished.

"You can text Jill." Karina added, collecting all the ingredients, and hiding the bodies. "I'm ready."

I hastily texted Jill, while Karina began warming up the cauldron.

"I wish we had some dry ice." Alyssa said, grumbling.

"Why?" Karina asked.

"It'd look cool. Obviously." I shrugged.

"Yes, but Jill's a forensic scientist. Part of showmanship is catering to your audience. If we make it too flashy, it might lose its magic." Karina took a moment. "That's a first for me, admittedly. Having to reign in the fancy bits."

Jill entered not long thereafter, and took a look at the cauldron. "Okay. Thanks. For... not including me in that part."

Karina nodded. "My pleasure. I've dealt with this sort of thing before."

"Let's get started." I said, with a deep breath.

Karina began adding things to the cauldron, and began whispering something in a language I didn't quite grasp.

"Is that…" Jill scrunched up her head. "It almost sounds familiar."

"She's chanting. She can't break the words. Everything has a specific order." Alyssa chastised.

"Don't interrupt, kid." I added, for good measure.

Karina finished chanting, before placing in the chameleon's heart, and frog eyes, before yanking a hair from Alyssa's head, her head, then mine, and tossing them all in.

"Ow!" I shouted.

"Don't interrupt." Jill chastised in a mocking manner.

Karina coughed, before a large tendril of smoke went up her nostrils.

She fell out of her wheelchair.

"Hey!" Alyssa said, moving to help Karina.

She held up a hand, before gesturing at me.

A circle of light appeared underneath me, and symbols that looked vaguely familiar drew themselves on the floor.

"That looks almost like the symbols on the mirror." I told her. "Maybe a bit?"

"They look Greek." Alyssa shook her head. "You need your eyes checked."

Karina coughed, and the smoke went down the hole in the floor that the previous spell cast.

It swirled back up, then surrounded me until it was absorbed in the light symbols on the floor.

Karina collapsed.

Then I fell to the floor in full Rusalka mode and groaned.

"Shit. Glad nobody else is in here." Alyssa said, collecting my hastily discarded lower garments.

"I don't think it worked." I grumbled.

Karina blinked, and rubbed the side of her face. "Something's... wrong. The magic. It didn't stay with me."

"Why not?" Jill asked, trying to hide her bewilderment at witnessing my tail for the first time. "Harmony, can I get you something to help with that?"

I bared my teeth, and hissed, before closing my eyes, and forcing myself to turn human again. "Something felt wrong."

"Was the light show you?" Alyssa asked Karina.

"What light show?" Karina awkwardly climbed back into her chair.

"There were symbols like the ones you drew on the mirror. They appeared in light. On the floor." I paused to get my pants on properly. "They seemed to eat the spell."

Karina narrowed her eyes. "You're a seawitch? SERIOUSLY? I kind of needed to know that!"

"Guppy? She doesn't have magic." Alyssa looked confused.

"The spell couldn't affect you to cast the tracking spell because your protection wards saw it as a threat and dissolved it." Karina scowled. "I've never even heard of a Rusalkan Seawitch. Rusalka are usually very exclusively outside of magical practices. Natural merfolk. Not veil entities. Never needed magic. Never developed access to magic."

"Wait. You're saying Guppy has her own protection spell?" Alyssa shook her head. "Wouldn't that have protected her from the vampire virus?"

"No." Karina shook her head. "Not unless she specifically warded against it." Karina blinked. "But. The virus may have inadvertently activated Seawitch genes that were dormant within her."

"What if you have Harmony try and cast the tracking spell, herself?" Jill suggested. "Maybe… her magic might work?"

Karina gestured to the cauldron. "Toss in the other frog eye, and the rest of the chameleon, then read the inscription on the page on the table. It's phonetic. Just read it as it's written."

I shrugged. "It couldn't hurt." I tossed in the ingredients, and took a breath. "Vock ay oooh rah ness. Vahn Lee wa eck."

"Hair." Karina instructed.

Alyssa pulled out one of my hairs, and tossed it in.

There was a white sizzle, and something tried to come out of the cauldron, but it was burnt away by a bright light.

Then, the whole room faded and there was a smell in the air. It was… overpowering. Indescribable, in that it smelled of nothing, and yet, still there.

"That's some protection spell." Karina looked bewildered. "It's working."

"Now what?" Alyssa asked.

"Follow however the spell is manifesting. You've got six hours. I'm going to have to rest." Karina gestured. "Go! You're on the clock."

"It's manifesting as a smell. Not a very nice one." I grumbled.

Alyssa gently led me to the door. "This isn't going to work if we drive."

"Use Vince's car. He drives a convertible." Jill suggested.

"Like Nash Bridges and-" Alyssa paused. "Nah, I can't make a fish joke out of that one."

"Before we jump, are you going to eat the rest of that frog?" I asked Karina.

"By all means, help yourself. Waste not, want not."

Nash Fishes

The tracking spell was an unusual experience. Everything else seemed dampened in contrast. Dandelions. Perfume. They all just faded into the background. It was like the scent of blood, except this time it smelled less distinctly of anything immediately recognizable.

We drove the car for hours. It seemed to be just random turns, following the smell. Pausing every now and then, to get our bearings. The clock ticked and we drove through most of the Greater Vancouver Regional District.

"You ever stop to think that maybe we're being deliberately misled?" Alyssa asked, a bit frustrated.

"The thought had occurred." I said as I got out of the car, and stared up the mountainside towards the village of Anmore. "Credit where it's due, we've been taken to all the fantastically scenic places, at least."

"Where's the smell coming from?" Alyssa stared over the Burrard Inlet, back towards the larger cities.

"Everywhere." I said, frustrated. "It's like… something is interfering, now. Like it knows it's being tracked?"

"Or the smell is everywhere because this is where it spends a large amount of time." Alyssa suggested.

I looked back up the mountainside, then back down towards Rocky Point park.

"Up the hill, or down the coast?" I asked, turning my attention back to the car.

"The coast seems most likely." Alyssa paused. "Which is why I'm thinking we might have better luck if we drive up the hill."

"Why?" I scrunched up my face. "That doesn't make any sense."

"It permits you to get a crossfix on the tracking spell." Alyssa retorted.

I looked out at the bay.

"Unless they're down there." I pointed out.

"Then… perhaps we should find a discreet place for you to go for a swim." Alyssa looked at her watch. "But you've got to make a decision, Guppy. We've wasted 4 hours already."

"Most of that in traffic." I added, with a groan. "I should have swam."

"Possibly." Alyssa narrowed her eyes. "Unless they aren't getting around by swimming."

"There's something… happening. Something weird." I shook my head.

Thunder rumbled. I looked up and blinked at the clouds.

"It was… sunny." Alyssa said, quietly. "Ten minutes ago. Not a cloud in the sky."

"That's because your magic is being dissipated into the air." A calm voice said from behind me.

I drew my weapon and turned around.

"Who are you supposed to be?" I asked. The gun was pointed at them out of instinct but they didn't seem bothered.

"I'm surprised you need that." The voice noted. It was… soft.

Quiet. Almost melodic. The woman it was attached to had a sturdy jaw, and an alluring set of lips. There was something incredibly attractive about the way she had her hair done up and it was in that exact second that my teeth bared, and my claws extended.

A siren knows a siren.

She raised her eyebrows, bemused.

"I can't seem to affect your friend." The woman said, looking towards Alyssa.

"Who is this?" Alyssa asked.

"She's a siren. I was expecting a seawitch." I hissed. "She's setting off every single one of my survival instincts. Watch yourself."

"Ahhhh. I see. I doubt that's a secret you'd share with just *anyone*. No wonder my magic can't affect her." The seawitch narrowed her eyes. "You *soulbound* a human to yourself. No other creature can ensnare her senses. The Siren Kiss."

"Listen, I'm going to level with you, I have not the slightest ink of an idea what you're on about." I hissed. "I tracked you here because you are trying to kill one of my closest friends."

"You're… not trained." The woman raised her eyebrows. "And to think! You have such incredible potential."

"You can tell what her magic potential is?" Alyssa interjected.

"I have never met a seawitch with potential this high. And yet… there." The woman gestured at my teeth. "Look. Pure instinct. You don't *think*. You *act*. You have less than zero capacity to actually USE it. Which means… You have an accomplice who is trained in magic." She narrowed her eyes. "Someone properly versed in sufficient seawitch magic to not only track me, but destroy my attempted deflection spell."

"Vincent Lasenza." I hissed, narrowing my eyes. "LET HIM GO."

The woman looked perplexed. "You should be able to save him. Strange."

"What's that supposed to mean?" Alyssa demanded.

"Why, you have everything you need at your disposal to undo the curse on him. Of course, his luck will invert to balance it. Some major loss or downfall." The woman tilted her head. "Except." She held up a finger. She looked bemused. "Can it be? Are you advised by a human witch? A seawitch would know how to undo it."

"Why tell me this?" I drew my weapon.

"That won't-" She paused, and stopped to examine the gun.

Strange music note sigils drew themselves along the side of my gun, sprinkled with droplets of water.

She raised her eyebrows. "So. It is you, after all. I was worried I hadn't found the right person." She laughed. "I tell you this, Harmony Williams, because I am forbidden from lying to you. Strange. Normally that requires a magical contract. The only *other* reason I can't be not honest with you is if you are somehow casting a truth field."

She looked down at my feet.

I frowned, and followed her gaze.

The Canadian Forces National Investigative Service logo was emblazoned in light at my feet.

"Truth, honor, and the Canadian way." The woman laughed. "I should have known. You are wielding your unusual magic in the line of duty. Probably for the very first time."

"Yes." Alyssa tilted her head. "Does that mean something?"

"Obviously. When you swear an oath to something, you are dedicating your morals and ethical code to it. Magic knows. It will reflect your core values. Who you are inside." The woman tilted her head. "A truth field. That's... fascinating instinctive magic. Hilariously, there actually *isn't* a spell on record that can be cast that forces people to speak the truth. Potions. Yes. Not a spell. That means you are either capable of *inventing* magic, or you aren't aware of the rules of magic, which means magic just does what you tell it."

"Same effect in the end." I shrugged.

"Indeed." The woman frowned. "However-" She held up her hands, and a black sigil drew between us.

I shot the tree behind her, and the gun flashed brightly.

"What-?" The woman blinked as her sigil vanished. "You can't DISPEL magic with a gun!"

"I'll dispel you next time." I said, with a very determined tone, and a squaring of shoulders to focus my aim on her head.

And then, she simply vanished into a puddle on the ground.

"Guppy?" Alyssa asked. "Your *gun* is magic?"

"I trust it to protect myself." I shrugged. "I'm sure Karina has some kind of explanation."

"We should ask her." Alyssa said, withdrawing her phone.

It began to rain.

"The smell. It's gone." I said, looking up at the clouds. I closed my eyes and let the rain drops dance on my face.

"She said your magic was dissipating into the air." Alyssa looked up. "Do you think this has something to do with it?"

"We should ask Karina. We're not going to track her anymore with this spell." I reiterated. "That woman. I wonder... who she was. I feel like I know her."

"She looked familiar."

"A little."

"Harmony… she looked like you."

"What? No way."

"Guppy, she knew your name."

A really long time ago

(Christmas, 1985)

Гармония

Christmas was 6 year old me's favorite thing. It was probably most 6 year olds' favorite thing. Dad had the tree up. He had brought me with him, so I could pick it out. I was big enough to have decorated it this year.

Dad had held me up high so that I could set the star on top the night before Christmas.

Now, though, it was Christmas MORNING.

I quietly crept down the stairs, but Granddad was already waiting for me.

He looked concerned. A woman sat opposite him.

He gave me the slightest glance, and the woman vanished from the chair.

He closed his eyes and winced.

He shook his eyes. "One day. When you're older." He said, quietly.

I didn't really care all that much.

I was *six*. It was *Christmas Morning*. There were *presents under the tree.*

Granddad followed my line of sight, and smiled. "Not until after breakfast. You know your grandmother's rules."

He paused, and looked around. "Though… I suppose one won't hurt."

He picked up a box, and patted the arm rest on his chair.

I hastily rushed to his side, making soft giggling noises.

"This is something special." He said, holding a finger to his lips. "You can't tell anyone where you got it."

"Okay." I said, impatiently.

He handed me the box, and I tore into it with the most enthusiasm I could manage. This was mysterious and special now.

Inside was a simple black and white photograph in an ornate frame.

I looked at it extremely disappointed. I had been hoping for the spanish doll I had been pointing at every single time we had gone through Zeller's* in the past two years.

*Zeller's is a registered trademark of the Hudson's Bay company even though they betrayed Canada by selling them to Target.

"This." Granddad said, pointing at the photo. "Was your mother and her mother, when she was your age. I know…" He paused. "I know you're still having a hard time with…"

"That's mommy?" I asked, suddenly losing all enthusiasm and excitement for the other gifts.

Granddad nodded. "When she was your age. Yes."

There was a silence between us, before I hugged the picture close.

Granddad took me on to his lap, and hugged me tighter.

Dad entered the room, bewildered by the sight.

Granddad nodded towards him. "Go show your father."

I quietly rushed over, and wrapped my arms around his legs, while holding the picture behind his back.

"What is it?" Dad asked.

I quietly held up the photo.

"Is that… Alena?" Dad paused. "And-" He paused to look at Granddad.

Granddad nodded. "I had to make some… unusual requests to get in touch."

"I can imagine." Dad shook his head, before picking me up, and holding me tight. "Listen here, little goldfish. This is a very rare treasure, okay? You be sure to keep that with you."

I nodded, and wrapped Dad in a deep hug. He smelled of wood chips. He always smelled of wood chips unless he just came back from being away.

"Who is this?" I asked, pointing at the other woman.

"That's your grandmother." Dad paused. "Her name was Althaia."

Dad quietly sat the photo down, and held me tightly against him, again, rubbing my back. "One day, little goldfish, you'll be ready to hear about that story."

Day 2

(Again)

Healing Song

The drive back to the naval base was quiet. I didn't have much to say. I was trying to rationalize everything that had just happened. It didn't make sense. It felt wrong.

The smells of the city were a welcome distraction. Bacon cheeseburgers. Greasy french fries. A Sharkbucks every 3 or 4 blocks imparted a constant undertone of burnt coffee. Car exhaust. People's perfumes and deodorants. The scent of a dozen different cuisines overwhelmed the other foods. Indian. Chinese. The world was a swirl of different smells, and they quickly began to overwhelm my less human senses.

"She was in your file." Alyssa said, quietly.

"What?" I blinked, focusing first on Alyssa's scent, before refocusing on her. "The seawitch?"

"We've seen her." Alyssa nodded. "In a black and white photo."

She dug through her bag, and withdrew the black file marked *Harmony Williams.*

"Here." She said, digging out the photo. "*Unidentified Rusalka.*"

"I expected a bit more from Military Intelligence." I said, with a bit of a laugh. "They really don't know who that is?"

"No. Apparently not." She shook her head. "She's just in this photo with…" She looked through the file. "*Alena Ignatova.* Your mother."

"She would be." I said, dryly. "Wow. What does the file say about her?"

"She's mysterious. Nobody ever identified her. She was sort of known to just appear and disappear, apparently." She frowned. "There are references to this woman protecting allied ships from german torpedoes in world war one, and she matches the description of countless women throughout history. She's listed as an unidentified guardian folk tale, outside of that-" Alyssa checked through the file. "-unless they're holding out on us, there's nothing."

"That's Althaia." I nodded to the photo. "At least... that's what Granddad said her name was."

"Your Grandfather knows her?" Alyssa blinked.

"Yeah. She's Alena's mother. My grandmother." I paused, as I stopped the car at a red light. "Wait, this is... her." I blinked. "But mom is grown in this photo?"

"Okay. Why is that surprising?" Alyssa asked.

"In my photo, my mother was just 6 or 7. Yet... Althaia hasn't aged between the two photos." I paused, tilting my head. "And I don't think she's aged any since."

"Althaia." Alyssa punched the name into her phone. "Greek, apparently."

"Not Russian?" I blinked.

Alyssa shook her head. "Not Russian." She paused. "Do you think she's a Rusalka? The notes in her file don't line up with the other Rusalka we've met."

"I have no idea." I shrugged. "She didn't smell Rusalka."

"She didn't?" Alyssa blinked.

"She smelled... almost seawitch." I focused on the traffic around us, and paused. "Not Cecaelia. Just a seawitch."

"And she heavily implied you're not just a Rusalka, either. That would make a kind of sense, wouldn't it?" Alyssa asked.

"She seemed bewildered by my abilities." I paused. "Though, in fairness, literally everyone has been, including Harmony Williams."

Alyssa chuckled at that. "Karina almost seems jealous."

"Alyssa, stop and think analytically. Rusalka can't have magic. Karina said as much." I paused.

Recognition dawned on Alyssa like she had just been hit by a clue by four and she turned sharply towards me. "She had magic, but she did seem particularly surprised by your magic."

"If she was my grandmother, wouldn't it make sense to her that I would have some version of her own magic?" I pondered.

"She did catch on really fast." Alyssa paused. "And she seemed to understand the rules of magic."

"And she seemed fully cognizant of the fact that I wasn't adhering to the expected rules of magic, after seeing it in action." I gave her a look.

"And if she was responsible for you having them, you'd think she'd have expected it." Alyssa took a moment. "You're thinking that's not Althaia."

"I'm thinking that if that is Althaia, she wasn't my grandmother." I retorted. "I only have fifth hand words about that."

"You aren't a hundred percent sure?" Alyssa asked, looking out over the river as we began to cross one of the bridges to the southern side of the Fraser river.

"Like I said. Granddad told me when I was 6." I shrugged. "I wish I knew more."

"We could ask him. His house is on the way back to the base, isn't it?" Alyssa paused. "But then again, supposedly you and Karina-"

"Have what it takes to save Vince." There was a silence as I stared up at the sky. "It's clear again. Strange."

"Not if the tracking spell is gone." Alyssa shook her head. "Two weeks ago, if you had told me I'd be using that term like it's a normal everyday phrase, I'd call you insane."

"Given the fact that I just had a standoff at the seawitch corral with someone claiming to be my grandmother, I'm still not sure I am not insane."

"Oh, you're Harmony Williams. Rusalkan magician of the deep who dresses up in human war colors and eats bad guys. Human psychology is of only limited use."

"Just enough to get in my pants."

"That does not require a psychology degree."

"Touché."

Ἀλθαία

The hospital room was quiet. Karina was asleep in her chair, next to Vince's bed.

"I just thought of a problem." Alyssa said, side-eyeing the sleeping woman.

"There's an antimagic field keeping Vince alive. We can't just try random spells that might work because he's going to decline rapidly." I nodded. "We're here for Karina. Vince is going to have to wait." I paused. "Though I'm not sure I should wake her. She looks exhausted."

"She's not used to casting magic." Alyssa pointed out.

"And the spell really gave her the old one-two punch." I agreed. "Still. There's a job to do."

I gently woke her up by putting my hand on her shoulder and she looked startled at the touch.

"Hey. The spell led us to something really wrong." Alyssa took a breath. "But it was heavily implied that a seawitch could easily undo this and the only thing Vince would suffer is some kind of loss."

"A misfortune curse? Is this amateur hour?" Karina groaned. "Did they attack you?"

"Very poorly. Guppy had another light show, and they suddenly couldn't lie. Her gun also shot a bullet that dispelled whatever spell she was casting on us." Alyssa paused, and withdrew my black file. "It looked like her."

"But you don't think it was?" Karina looked surprised.

"She's my grandmother, but the person we met seemed surprised by both the caliber of my abilities, and my apparent unique skill of inventing magic." I closed my eyes to focus on Karina's scent. "No. She wasn't even close to cecaelia in smell. She wasn't Rusalka, either."

"Who was your grandfather?" Karina was suddenly very intrigued by the photo.

"Mom never said. I'm not sure she knew. If that woman isn't a Rusalka, though-" I pointed out.

"That would imply you don't have a grandfather." Karina nodded. "Rather, a child born of magic. Theoretically possible if you're powerful enough and given your own capacity, the theory has quite a bit of backup."

"You think my mother came out of one of your seawitch vials?" There was a great deal more surprise in my voice than the events of the last day should have left it with.

"What? No. Ink, no." She laughed. "That's not seawitch magic. It would take someone more powerful. We can, technically, but the child wouldn't inherit any of our abilities. Creation magic is really difficult to mimic and is rarely done correctly. Not counting you, there is exactly one historical incident on record of that happening and 99% of the residents of this planet wouldn't believe you if you explained that event. The fact that you're using magic neither side of your family has previously displayed suggests it was a gift from a god or a demigod. Like the child made of clay, or Athena being an exceedingly angry pimple that didn't like staying on Zeus' forehead."

"So... Mom was a gift to Althaia?" I scrunched up my face, trying to riddle out Karina's words.

"Not quite. From. A gift from Althaia. Supposedly, there was a

Greek woman of some renown with an incredible ability to heal. So much so that Althaia came to mean *healer.*" Karina closed her eyes. "She was a queen, I think. The history around her has always felt suspiciously covered up. Anyway, the gift would be you, not her. Otherwise, you wouldn't be as powerful."

"You think Althaia is an ancient Greek goddess?" Alyssa blinked.

"Demigoddess? Goddess? Who knows. There are a lot of gods and demigods whose stories were destroyed or rewritten by the victors of fights." Karina took a breath. "Ink, Medusa is routinely written to be a villain to this day. Historical record is always written from the perspective of misogynistic male victors."

"But she survived. Otherwise Guppy wouldn't have happened." Alyssa surmised.

"And then you almost died." Karina snapped her fingers. "You actually did die. Your soul was prepared to leave your body. It would have gone wherever beings made of magic go and it was translated into the magic you were made of, then forcibly drawn back into your body when the virus animated you again."

"That can happen?" Alyssa blinked. "That sounds improbable."

"Theoretically? Yeah." Karina nodded. "There's a lot of literature on people who die on surgical tables coming back to life with different memories, abilities, and things that make their life worth living. Wherever we go when we die, it refines our soul, somehow."

"So Althaia might actually be surprised by my abilities, should she witness them?" I paused. "No. That's wrong. Isn't it? Why is that wrong?"

"You're learning fast. If your soul reverted back to the magic Althaia used to create you, she'd recognize it easily and instantly because it would be hers. That's not to say she could defend against it. Her own protection spells would be also made out of you and anything offensive you did against her would be unhindered by her other magics in much the same way you used the tracking spell to follow Vince's curse." Karina paused. "But that would also mean it would be one hell of a shock, even for a full blood sea-witch. Gods can invent magic. You were saying something-"

"Guppy created some kind of light show that created a field where people had to speak the truth." Alyssa filled in.

"A truth serum in magic field form?" Karina's eyebrow went up. "That's definitely... Fae magic? Maybe? Unusual, for certain. I couldn't do it, and I can only think of maybe three non-deity and non-Fae entities that might be able to. And one of them might not actually exist."

"So either Guppy used deity magic or she invented magic." Alyssa took a moment to process that. "She actually might be able to test magic to save Vince in here."

"Karina has an antimagic field up." I pointed out.

"Doesn't apply to most demonic or deific magic." Karina shook her head. "Just human witchcraft of varying types and most veil magic. Hell, some nature magic will ignore it."

I was accustomed to being the slowest one in the room but somehow, it felt like I really should have caught that without explanation and I looked away to hide my embarrassment.

"The thing that did this can't be Althaia if I'm able to cast magic in this room." I had trouble finding my more commanding voice. It just wasn't there.

"That's a good catch. Now, if all it's going to take is a misfortune curse, I have one of those in my bookbag." Karina noted, grabbing a bag off the back of her chair. "Do you read Farsi?"

"No." I gave her a confused look.

"German?" Karina asked, shuffling books in the bag.

"Vaguely." I nodded.

"Here. Read this." She handed me a book.

I flipped it open, and the lights flickered.

Karina looked up. "Storm magic?"

"Your tracking spell wore off in the form of a rain storm." Alyssa nodded.

"That makes enough sense." Karina laughed. "She is a siren. The magic she uses, intentionally or not, would be refined by whom and what she is."

I paused on a page, and frowned.

"What?" Karina asked.

"If I've got this translated right, this is a prayer to a god who cures diseases." I held it up.

"Apollo. Roughly. Germanic pagan beliefs were very roughly mismatched between Nordic, Celtic, and Roman gods." Karina grabbed the book. "What? Are you thinking of asking him for help?"

"I'm thinking that if I'm the magical granddaughter of some Greek goddess named Healing, Apollo is probably in some way related to her." I retorted.

"Family favors?" Alyssa looked surprised. "You think that might work?"

"What have we got to lose?" Karina handed the book back. "You can always try misfortune curses later."

I read through the prayer, and closed my eyes.

Apollo, healer of men and beasts, vanquisher of plague and injury, I pray to you in my hour of need-

The lights went out.

The mirror that had Karina's antimagic spell on it shattered.

Vince sat up straight.

I opened my eyes, darting my attention to the sound of breaking glass.

"Harm?" Vince asked, putting a hand to his head. "I just had the most messed up dream."

Karina looked absolutely mystified.

Alyssa wrapped Vince in a tight hug.

"Your file is so *incredibly* wrong about literally every aspect of your past." Karina whispered.

"I don't care." I laughed.

"I do. Commander, if literally anyone else in military intelligence finds out you have access to this kind of thing, you'll never breathe free air again. They'll torment, torture and experiment on you. What you just did is a literal miracle." Karina hissed.

"Would they actually be able to do it?" I gave her an amused smile.

"Well-" She looked towards the mirror shards. "No. Probably not."

"Who would?" I asked, looking out the window behind her, admiring the second unexpected rainfall of the day.

"Anyone who knows how to hurt gods, I guess. Demons. Other gods. God hunters. Jinn and angels." Karina paused. "THAT'S IT!"

"That's what?" Alyssa turned her attention to Karina from Vince.

"Whatever that was has been evaluating us. Evaluating my magic in the armory. Evaluating your magic during your confrontation. They knew you or someone like me would be the ones to come for them." Karina looked very worried.

"So they can figure out the easiest way to kill us." I finished.

"They're doing to us what we've been doing to them. Testing. Investigating. Deducing." Alyssa paused. "Some kind of... magic hunter?"

"No. Magic and monster hunters can't pull off things of this magnitude unless they're not human. This is either a god, a demigod, or some kind of-" Karina looked at me intently. "In the form of a familiar but mysterious loved one. Magic that mimics other creatures perfectly but can't appropriately mimic deific magic. Ability to reshape reality to give people wishes as though they were a sea-witch or a fairy godmother."

"You know what it is."

"And how to kill it."

"Well, fish hooks, that didn't take long."

It was quiet in the morgue. We all stared at the collected piles of books, pages, and notes strewn across one of the morgue tables.

"The only thing I can pin this down definitively as is a Trickster." Karina explained, gesturing at the files.

"Makes enough sense." Alyssa noted, reading one of the pages.

"I got a question." Vince chimed in. "Why this? Why are they pretending to be something else? This is a pretty messed up game they're playin'."

"That." Karina pointed at him with an annoyed look before her face softened. "Is actually clever. It's the only thing missing."

"What's missing?" Jill frowned. "I think we've got everything there is to know about this thing." She picked up a paper. "This is very well researched."

"Basic investigation 101. Every crime has a motive." I filled her in.

Jill froze. "Wow. And Vince got it before me."

"There's no reason to do any of this." Karina agreed.

"Of course there is." I retorted.

"Oh?" Karina glared. "Fill me in."

"Not me." I gestured towards her. "You already did. Alyssa, back me up, here."

Alyssa smirked a bit. "Quite right. Look at the victims, first. All military. We've had no reports of civilians affected. The timing?

Vince being a target? You've got to step back and profile the crime." She gestured around the room. "Us. Think about it. Harmony just cracked a case that seemed impossible. Doctor Zehlendorf stopped a plague that could have killed millions. Our effects on the world, for the very first time, have an astonishingly massive ripple effect."

"The victims are all military. They are all also within the GVRD. They literally were first cursed *while we were stopping the virus.*" I added. "We would be investigating their deaths. The methodology?" I gestured at Karina.

"Personal. Meaning I would be inspired to more directly take over the cases because they hit too close to home." Karina winced. "SON OF A SHARK."

"What?" Vince paused. "Oh. Hold on."

"The motive is us." Jill said, simply. "We did something that should have taken years in days."

"We broke the way things were supposed to be." Karina nodded. "Well. You did."

"You were added as a catalyst. Someone…" I scrunched up my face. "Someone wants me to… what?"

"Reach your full potential." Alyssa finished. "She said as much. She was disappointed you weren't trained with your magic and she was right. You cured Vince's curse."

"The motive is me." I blinked. "All of this."

Jill hastily grabbed my arm. "It isn't your fault."

"You're not the one doing this anymore than the one who developed that virus." Alyssa added.

I closed my eyes and took a breath.

"You saved me, Harm." Vince said, quietly. "That's who you are.

Without you, I'd be gone."

I gave the slightest trace of a smile at that.

The room glowed bright, and symbols drew themselves under everyone in the room.

"What does it say?" Vince asked, looking down.

"Guardian." Alyssa pointed at my feet. "Protector. Analyst. Healer. Daughter." She paused, confused at the symbol under Karina's chair. "Sister?"

"News to me." Karina held up her hands.

"Not literal." Vince shook his head. "In the same sense that everyone in the trenches with you is your brother or sister."

"I'm teaching her magic. Like an older sibling teaching one soccer or-" Karina began.

"How to defend our family." I interrupted. "I don't like this game."

"Why the symbols?" Jill asked. "We all pretty much knew-"

"Defining sigils." Karina interrupted. "Protection spells, I think. Sigil magic."

"We're going to hunt down one of the most infamous and consistent irritants in human history." I nodded. "You honestly think my heart would leave you undefended?"

"Biggest?" Vince scrunched up his face.

"The Trickster is a consistent figure through most of human mythology." Karina shook her head. "I'm catching on. Sorry. I forget that you're going to need hand-holding through this. There are indigenous communities here that consider the Trickster their creation god. Protagonist. Antagonist. Sidewaystagonist. No matter what strange spin they put on it, there is a Trickster in just about every culture on earth."

"And you're thinking... what?" Vince paused. "They're all the same person?"

"And they're here." Karina nodded.

"Hunting me, specifically." I finished.

"WHY?" Vince demanded. "You're a target. Not a motive."

"Order." A soft voice said from the door.

"What?" I turned.

The same face. This time, though. She smelled like... me.

"You're... the real one." I stated.

"Yes, little one." Althaia nodded. "And it would seem you are making an impact in the world in ways fate did not dictate."

"And a Trickster has an issue with that?" Vince's hand was less than subtly going for his sidearm.

"That will not work." The woman shook her head. "I am not here to harm. You ask a wise question. Normally a Trickster would love unexpected chaos."

"Except." Alyssa gestured at me. "She fixed the chaos."

"She brought order. She was good. Kind. A protector that saved countless lives slated to die." Althaia nodded.

"The Trickster is targeting me because..." I closed my eyes, and sighed. "Because I am the Guardian. The order. The safety. The one thing they despise more than anything else."

"The absence of treachery." Karina blinked. "An anti-trickster?"

"No." Alyssa shook her head. "Harmony is always Harmony."

"It was never about anything personal." Althaia nodded. "As with her mother, and myself, all she wants is to heal the world."

"And a Trickster would hate that." Karina laughed.

"Because no matter what they do, they're going to end up opposed to you." Vince filled in.

"This is them choosing to pick the fight on their terms." I nodded. "Home field advantage."

"And they will have guessed where you got your powers by now." Althaia nodded.

"Except." I held up a hand to Alyssa.

"Guppy used magic in ways Magic isn't supposed to work." Alyssa smirked.

"And that is your weapon, child.

The chaos intended to bring order."

<h1 style="text-align:center">Aneris</h1>

It was dark. I sat quietly on the porch swing next to Granddad. He took a moment to light a pipe and stare up at the sky.

"I figured you would meet her, eventually." He said, taking a moment to inhale deeply, before blowing smoke into the air. "What did she tell you?"

"Very little." I took a breath. "Only that most of what we've guessed is correct."

"Not entirely." Granddad took a moment to draw in the smoke hanging in the air. "You aren't technically your father's daughter."

I gave him a surprised look. "What the hell do you mean by that?"

"It'll be a lot easier if you take a moment to let me finish." Granddad laughed. "A very long time ago, your mother discovered that she couldn't have children. It is not as though they didn't try for many years."

He tilted his head up at the sky. "Your mother prayed to many. She searched through dozens of texts. No seawitch would talk to her. No sorcerers. No fairy godmothers. The world cared not for a Rusalkan woman who was not fated to have children."

"But I am here." I pointed out.

"And, indeed, so you are." He chuckled. "She came to us. The woman from the sky, healer of the lost." He took a moment to draw out Althaia's greek script name in the air with his finger. "She was certain of something… wrong with the world. She said that the fate had to be changed, but no one else was willing to do the job. It sounds familiar, I'm sure."

I looked down at the porch. "Very much so." My voice was much quieter than I intended.

"She defied the fate of the world, and she changed just one thing. A child unbound by the rules of the way the world should be." He leaned back against the porch swing. "Althaia gave your mother the gift she could not give herself or your father." He turned his head. "You."

"That makes a disturbing amount of sense." I twirled my fingers through the smoke, and for just a second, the smoke swirled around my finger, and formed into the symbol that had glowed under me when the protective sigils formed. "Karina said that when the virus killed me, I reverted to the magic that made me."

"And in the world's scary moment, when two of the most terrifying viral infections in the world break out in the same year." Granddad gestured around. "You and the people whose lives you have changed. The people you've saved. The people who stand up when others don't. You made them guardians."

"I changed their fates." It was a simple explanation, and it made me realize exactly how shocking this was.

"And the world shines bright." He frowned as his pipe went out. "Frustrating." He added, dryly. "I'm out, and your mother won't let-"

I held out a package of fresh tobacco that I had concealed in my jacket.

Granddad took it without a word.

"You think this was her plan, all along?" I asked.

"Althaia? I doubt it." He chuckled. "When she gave me that photo of your mother, she explained that a very long time ago, a woman had broken from her expected fate, and in so doing, saved Althaia's life. She didn't elaborate, but apparently the woman saved the world from something quite terrible."

"And that matters… how?" I prodded.

"She told me, when she gave me that photo, that she had made a promise to that woman." Granddad took a moment to relight his freshly refilled pipe. "And that promise was simple. The world had suffered wars beyond any reckoning prior and she was afraid that war was getting out of hand, like chaos had, before. She promised that when the world looked at its bleakest. When the darkness overshadowed the good. She would defy fate, just as this woman had, to give the world a fighting chance."

I frowned, and stared up at the stars. "I was never supposed to be here."

"And neither was the virus you stopped. Nor the strange magic that surrounds your life, now." He laughed. "Magic, it seems, is not only real, but gaining against reality."

"Not all of it's bad. I've seen some magic used for great good." I looked down at the empty ring finger on my left hand in thought. "Lauren could never be, could she?"

"Harmony, you were never supposed to be. I imagine the fates of the world took some pretty great offense to you having a child." Granddad shook his head. "That doesn't give them the right, though."

"The right?" I withdrew Lauren's photo from my wallet. "That doesn't give them the right to take lives." I ran a finger along the photo with a slight smile. "That doesn't give them the right to take light away from people who need it."

"Just as whatever it is you are chasing does not have the right to take the lives it has taken." Granddad took a deep breath. "Somebody once told me that the world is filled with darkness, hatred, spite, and cruelty, like the cold uncaring vastness of the sky."

He pointed towards a bright star in the sky. "But look. Polaris." He laughed. "The northern star, long used as a guide point for those lost in the world. There will always be room for people to bring light to those who are bereft of it. You made your choice as to who you would become."

I leaned back against the porch chair, and stared at the star, thoughtfully. "Ursa Minor."

"The little bear." Granddad nodded.

"How fitting." I laughed.

"How so?" He looked briefly confused, before his eyes brightened as he focused on another constellation. "The mother bear. Hah. Yes, I suppose it is."

"Did she tell you anything else, back then?" I turned to him, before getting up.

"Only that when the time came, and you were ready to know the truth, you'd have already figured it out, and what to do next." He shrugged. "She had a fondness for the enigmatic flare."

"So does the thing we're hunting." I took a moment to offer a morbid chuckle. "I'll give it to them both, they certainly were made for eachother."

"I suppose so." Granddad paused. "Though, I'll give Althaia this much." He looked up at the stars with a smile. "When she throws a rock to alter the river of fate, she certainly knows how to throw the right rock."

"No." I gave a bit of a laugh. "To quote a friend, that's not luck. That's Harm."

"Hah. I suppose that's fair." Granddad took a moment to consider things. "She did say she was giving the world a fighting chance. If she had something specific in mind, I'd imagine she'd have made it more obvious."

"Why mom, though?" I looked up, suddenly. "Why help my mother?"

"Because she saved people. When the others were content to do as Rusalka do, she saw the world devolving into war, and she went into the waters, and saved any and every sailor she could." Granddad laughed. "For the same reason your father loved her. Hell, that's how they met. She pulled him out of the Pacific."

"Althaia… chose mom. Not dad?" I gave him a look of understanding.

"She chose the Guardian, Harmony." Granddad chuckled. "Because she would give the world a gift of one who heals by protecting."

"Is that why my mother gave me the name that she did?" I raised my eyebrows. "A harmony. Chaotic sound brought to order."

"The rock, when the world is in a hard place." Granddad laughed. "You've never been particularly gentle."

"A song doesn't have to be gentle. There are heavy metal bands." I pointed out.

Granddad gave me a knowing smile.

"I believe you know what to do, yes?" He asked.

"A guitar solo?"

"Don't forget the rest of the band."

"Good night, Vancouver!"

"We're in Richmond, little pup."

"Oh, like the rest of the world knows where to find Richmond on a map."

Day 3

March 16, 2020

*Golden Ears provincial park,
British Columbia*

Flotsam and Copyright avoidance

The remote area of the park was not particularly wheelchair accessible. It made getting Karina to a place where it was safe to practice magic of this caliber a bit irritating with half a kilometer involving Alyssa carrying her wheelchair, while I carried her.

"This would be a lot easier if we had fancy teleportation magic like they have on T.V." Alyssa grumbled.

"Hush, the wheelchair only weighs 20 kilos." I grumbled.

"Are you saying I need to lose some weight?" Karina asked in a pouty tone. There was an uncomfortable moment where arms tightened around my chest.

"Hey!" I exclaimed while trying to knock her with the back of my head.

What happened instead was not anything so graceful. A bright rune glowed between us, and she was knocked off me, onto the ground.

"Alright, alright!" Karina grumbled. "Ow, son of a shark."

"Hey, that's what you get for pissing off the mystery white light of destiny." Alyssa shrugged, unfolding the chair. "You can make it from here."

"Can I?" Karina asked, looking at the landscape dubiously.

"I really hope so." Alyssa added, shaking her head.

"Fair enough." She took a moment to stare out at the view below us. "I've never seen this before."

Turning to see what caught her attention, the cities that made up 'Vancouver' sprawled out in front of us.

"Wow." Alyssa tilted her head. "I-"

"Almost as good as watching this city grow in front of you as the ship you are on pulls into port after a long deployment." I put a hand on Karina's shoulder. "I'll give you this much. You might not be the most clever of trailblazers, but you sure know how to pick a view."

"Even if it did take most of the day to get up here." Alyssa added, with a slightly irritated voice.

"Listen, this isn't the kind of magic we can do in an armory." Karina grumbled.

"I didn't mind. I've done worse." I shrugged.

"You did not." Alyssa laughed.

"Oh, yeah? *You* try climbing a 50 meter high sand hill while trying to avoid enemy fire in 46 degree desert weather." I retorted. "With 20 kilos of gear."

There was silence.

"Afghanistan was MEAN." Karina agreed. "This is pretty tame, in contrast."

"You know what? I really shouldn't try and doubt her anymore." Alyssa looked behind us. "Hey, you know that feeling like you're being watched?"

I took a moment to focus back on the here and now, and took a sniff. "We're alone, barring the squirrel 7 meters away, and a very concerned bumble bee."

"Concerned?" Karina scrunched up her face. "How-"

"Pheromones. Danger smell. You give them out. I give them out. Bees give them out. You'd be surprised how many creatures are capable of expressing their distress and observing yours that way." I interrupted. I moved her chair closer to her, before looking around. "Are we remote enough yet?"

Karina looked around, before focusing on a small pool of water. "Well, if this thing is tuned to water, I quite like the idea of it being contained. Let's get started."

She placed several disgusting, slimy, or delicious smelling tupperware containers in a simple triangle design, and then began muttering something in what sounded somewhere close to a nordic dialect.

A lightning blast struck the center of the triangle, knocking Karina back, before causing it to rain.

"INK! HARMONY, PUT THAT DAMN THING ON A LEASH!" Karina shouted.

"Oh, yes, because I WOULDN'T HAVE ALREADY DONE THAT IF I KNEW HOW!" I grumbled, before backing away a fair distance. "Alright, try it now." I added, crossing my arms and taking a seat on a convenient stump.

A squirrel was sitting next to the stump, and he looked up at me in an accusatory stare.

I stood up, and realized there were seeds on the stump. I quickly brushed the seeds off my posterior. "Sorry about that." I told the squirrel. "Didn't mean to steal your food."

The squirrel continued to stare at me annoyed.

"HARMONY!" A distressed voice came from behind me. I twirled and rushed, drawing my weapon. The storm clouds returned.

Alyssa and Karina were trying to fend off two very angry snakes.

A lightning blast struck between the snakes and myself. I aimed my gun, and gave them a siren-faced glare.

"Thank god for those protection sigils." Alyssa said, standing in front of Karina.

"Must be nice to have one." Karina added, unamused.

"Listen, you're the one who was bitching about my magic interfering with your-" I paused just long enough to shoot at a snake that lunged. "-Can we do this later?"

"My bullets aren't doing much good." Alyssa frowned. "I'm down to 4."

"I didn't even hear the bullets." There was a moment as the three of us returned our attention to the snakes. "Ah. Trying to keep things from me."

"Their skin is too tough. The bullets just glance off." Karina looked between the closest snake and Alyssa. "This was not what I was expecting."

"Let's try this." I set my gun back into the holster, and lunged forward at the snake with claws extended.

This confused the snake, and caused it to fall backwards.

Karina dropped a rock on it's head.

There was an unexpectedly satisfying crunch.

I turned to the other snake, focusing on it, and nothing else.

It became increasingly agitated, and lunged towards me. I grabbed it by the neck with my left hand, drew my gun, shoved it into its mouth and fired upwards.

There was a brief hissing noise before the snake fell limp.

"That was gutsy, Guppy." Alyssa looked more than a bit annoyed.

Karina was silent, hiding behind Alyssa, cowering in fear.

"Hey. Easy." Alyssa turned, confused by the woman's fear and clinging.

"It's alright." I took a moment to recollect myself, staving off the more feral aspects of being in nearly full siren mode by focusing on Alyssa. "Easy." I added, this time with less sharp teeth.

"That-" Karina whispered. "-you-"

"Yes." I nodded. "If it makes you feel any better, you weren't in any danger."

"Didn't feel like it." Karina said, still cowering. "You were... scary."

"She never would have hurt you." Alyssa reassured her. "This is the Harmony that saved the world from a vamprizing virus."

"She was all... shark smelling. There was nothing human or rusalka about her left." Karina settled back in her chair.

"That's new." Alyssa looked confused. "Isn't it?"

"We don't really have outside knowledge. I know the others didn't smell like that when they were in fight or flight mode." I shrugged. "Might just be me."

Karina gave me a haunted look as I stepped closer. I gently placed a hand on her shoulder. "Easy." I knelt down next to her. "You're not in any danger. I know our magic clashes, but I would never intentionally harm you outside of gentle ribbing."

"Why don't you affect her like this?" Karina looked towards Alyssa.

"Alyssa is marked with a siren scent." I pointed out. "She's... safe. Always. Safe. And she knows it. Her body doesn't react this way because she's seen me like this before, and I was still me. I could never hurt her."

Karina turned back towards me, searching my face. "Do you know why my spell didn't work?" She tilted her head.

"How the ink should I know?" I gave her a surprised look. "You're the expert, Karina."

"It did work." Alyssa pointed out.

"How so?" Karina looked back at her even more surprised than I was.

"Snakes are very commonly associated with the trickster." Alyssa pointed out. "That was in your books."

"That's where the bible got the idea of Samael being a snake from." Karina looked thoughtful. "You don't think-"

"I really hope not." I laughed. "I'm not quite sure a square dance with the devil is high on my bucket list."

"Who even square dances anymore?" Alyssa frowned.

"It's an idiom." I shook my head. "Karina. You were speaking in something nordic sounding."

Karina's face lit up with recognition. "And I was using the rune for trickster, which is also commonly associated with Loki. Or vice versa. I'm rusty on Nordic runes."

"For shame." I gave her a fake condescending look.

There was a rumble of thunder and then the clouds cleared around us, leaving a late sunset.

"You seriously do dissipate magic with thunderstorms." Karina looked amused, as she looked up at the clear sky.

"And she wouldn't hurt you." Alyssa reiterated.

I looked back towards the shape of the attempted spell work, and then I frowned.

"What if it wasn't my magic that interrupted your spell?" I asked.

"What do you mean?" Karina looked up, intrigued by this statement.

"Well, the first time, it simply struck you back, but once I wasn't nearby, it seemed to respond with a directly offensive line of response." I pointed out. "What if the spell was being deflected from the other side?"

"And then attack dogs were sent to stop it when I restarted." Karina looked around, thoughtfully. "And Alyssa did feel like she was being watched."

"Alternatively, Harmony's magic realized that there was an attempt to counter attack your spell." Alyssa suggested.

"More likely than Harmony's theory." Karina admitted. "Particularly given how volatile the spell manifested."

She took a moment. "Her magic wasn't trying to cause harm." She added.

"I told you." I took a breath. "What if I try and cast that?"

"I wouldn't." An irritated voice said, from behind me.

I twirled about, gun drawn.

A man gave a bemused look. "You remind me of an old friend."

"Who the hell are you?" I demanded.

"I am Loki and I am REALLY annoyed by your cursed truth field." He gave a distasteful look at the ground under me.

"If you'd have just told the truth, I wouldn't need it." I pointed out.

"She said." Alyssa began.

"To the God of Lies and Treachery." Karina added.

Loki gave a slight smirk at that.

"Yeah, yeah, yeah." I grumbled.

The leading man

Loki offered a slow clap, as he walked closer. "I must say, you all catch on to puzzles a lot faster than I expected." He gestured around the area. "You're a lot better at finding breathtaking views than my last protege, as well. The outskirts of France and Germany were not the most wonderful views when you traveled as a vagrant." He paused. "Though that trip to Rotterdam was almost as nice."

"What the hell are you on about?" It was a simple enough question. I wasn't particularly in a mindset to quibble over polite discussion. "And why the hell did you kill those people?"

"*I* didn't." Loki chuckled. "They knew that if they failed to do a specific task, magic would take their lives instead."

"What do you mean, *protege*?" Karina tilted her head. "Was this some kind of test?"

"You killed 6 people and almost killed a seventh for a *test*?" Alyssa added.

"In reverse order, yes, yes, and-" Loki paused to stare at me thoughtfully. "Well. This isn't the first time I encouraged someone onto a specific path. You may be surprised by this, but I actually do not want to cause you any harm."

"Funny way of showing it, you slippery eel." Alyssa grumbled.

"Did she just make an ocean joke?" Karina blinked.

"A plus execution." I paused to give it some thought. "I quite like that one."

"Hello, I'm still standing here." Loki gave an irritated look.

"Oh, someone doesn't like it when we segue or take the limelight off of his nefarious deeds." Alyssa paused. "Narcissistic personality? Borderline sociopathy? We call that Borderline Personality Disorder, now."

"It was necessary." Loki frowned. "If you would actually ask me your stupid questions, you'll figure it out."

"Why the hell are you here?" I reiterated.

"Ah, yes." Loki clapped his hands together. "Delightful. To the point. I am here because the world is in danger."

"From WHAT?" Alyssa scrunched up her face. "What possible reason do you have to take 6 lives?"

"Magic." Loki said, simply. "Humans are well known to be particularly unstable with it. You've seen what happens." He gestured around. "That's why we're here. Magic is seeping into this world in ways it was never supposed to."

"And this has happened before?" Karina blinked. "I don't think I've got records of this happening before."

Loki held out his hands, and four books hovered between us. *Snow White, Cinderella, Little Red Riding Hood, Pinocchio.*

"Stories?" Karina frowned. "Wait. No. Imagination."

"Exactly." Loki paused, and the books vanished. "Human imagination and the magic created for this world are dangerous. Having that magic leech into this world... has had disastrous effects before. Dragons, particularly."

"Dragons." Alyssa repeated.

"Usually someone got around to killing them." Loki paused once more. "Usually."

"You pushed someone on the path to fix it?" I asked. "Before?"

"Several times, actually. I can't count the amount of times, and through the number of different ways it's happened." Loki looked briefly thoughtful. "There was a woman in Egypt who helped me once. Daughter of a pharaoh. The others are slightly less believable."

"Why do you care?" Karina asked. "You're the trickster. This should delight you."

"Are you *insane*?" Loki asked, suddenly shocked. "The entire universe slowly being flooded with creatures and people from your mythology? Even I have limits. Your magic once caused a war so impressive it afflicted the 9 realms with a near apocalypse. That's... not treachery. That's straight up suicide. My birth parents were literally killed in that war."

"But this is supposed to happen? Fate allowed it?" I frowned. "That doesn't make sense."

"Oh, it never does. Usually, it takes someone unbound from fate by an event, or an encounter with a being from the other side of the veil, and then something truly *impossible* happening, causing a tear in the wall between what is real and what is veiled." Loki laughed. "Fate hates it. She tries to force the melded world to follow a different path every time, but every time someone unbound from fate also ends up sealing it."

"I've heard enough." I said, focusing my gun on him. "You had no right to take those lives."

"You're hardly the first person I've tried to push onto this path, and they definitely weren't the first I've taken in this quest." Loki retorted. "I thought heroes believed in sacrifices for-" He paused to do air quotes. "*The Greater Good.*"

"Oh, fish sticks." Alyssa muttered.

"What?" Loki demanded.

"There are lines you don't cross. Killing people to achieve your goal? That's a soldier mentality. I've been one of those before." My finger twitched on the trigger. "I have some history with killing. I hardly have cleaner hands than you. That being said, I don't kill people I don't have to kill. Killing you? That would save lives, too, wouldn't it?"

Loki took a step back, suddenly uncomfortable. He withdrew two short swords made of ice out of the air.

Storm clouds brewed above us, and the swords simply dissolved into the air, as it began to rain.

"That is a neat trick." Loki said, looking between us. "I have an alternate method." He gestured, and a ghostly image of Lauren drifted between us. An elderly woman I didn't recognize. Karina's tentacles began to glow. "Wishes are easy enough to grant."

There was a moment.

A cold, dark, shocked moment, where I stood frozen.

This man was offering to return my daughter to me.

The temptation was incredibly overpowering.

And then there was a sharp pain in my back.

The Loki in front of me vanished.

"Of course, I've never been known to play fair." Loki tossed a bloodied knife into my vision. "Through your rib cage, straight through your lungs and heart. No more talking. No more threatening. No more irritating self righteousness. No. More. You."

He turned to Alyssa and Karina.

"She really should have taken me up on that." He added, laughing.

Thump.

Thump.

My vision darkened.

I couldn't breathe.

My heart stopped echoing in my head.

I couldn't move. The pain was excruciating.

And then.

Commander Harmony
Williams will not return.

The End.

...

. . .

?

Thump.

Thump.

113

Thump.

En Garde

For just a second, I saw Lauren again. She smiled quietly, and shook her head.

I gave her a confused look. I still couldn't speak.

It was dark. There was nothing else around us.

She threw something at me. It landed next to me, which was good because I couldn't get up.

I reached for it, wincing at the strange pain.

A photo of her, Victor, and me.

But I was in uniform, and both of them were dressed for their funerals.

"I love you, mommy." She whispered.

Thump. Thump. Thump. The sound began to thunder around us. I covered my ears.

And then I opened my eyes.

Laying on the ground, staring at the knife.

"I suppose you two don't serve any purpose anymore." Loki paused. "I was expecting more, for some reason."

Gun shots. One. Two. Three. Four.

A fizzled attempt at a spell that made a hissing noise.

"Is that the best you've got?" Loki laughed. There was a moment before there was the sound of ice shattering.

"What-?" Alyssa asked. "The sigils?"

"They shouldn't be working." Karina said, quietly. "Unless."

Everything was cold. I couldn't feel the pressure of the ground against my body. I couldn't feel pain. I couldn't feel anything.

I bared my teeth. My sharpened nails dug into the ground. My lower extremities suddenly forgot how to be bipedal, but it didn't matter. Not right this second.

All I had in me was rage.

I didn't understand why. I recognized that my brain was in a familiar feral state that I had once woken up in. I made an angry screech.

Loki turned, raising an eyebrow.

I lunged off the ground at him, and tackled him to the ground.

He vanished, and attempted to stab me in the back again.

He was knocked backwards by a lightning strike.

I took a breath, and turned towards him.

"You were dead." Loki frowned. "How is this possible?"

"Technically, she was kind of undead before that." Alyssa pointed out.

"Historically, the undead are really hard to kill." Karina added in a helpful tone.

I didn't have any clever words. I just hissed angrily at him.

He vanished, and suddenly there were four of him, surrounding me.

I screamed. Loudly. Animalistic. There was a thunderclap, and three of them were struck by lightning, causing them to vanish.

I focused on my tail in annoyance, and after a few failed attempts, I was able to stand up.

"Harmony, you're white as a ghost." Alyssa frowned.

"Probably not the best choice of words." Karina retorted.

"Ah. So you *are* trained in your magic, but not when you're properly in control of yourself." He looked briefly puzzled. "How is it that I can't freeze your blood?"

"Don't. Have. Any." I hissed.

"What?" Loki looked puzzled.

Alyssa began laughing hysterically.

"What's so funny?" Karina asked.

"You have some." I hissed at him.

Loki took several steps backwards.

"Vampirizing Fasciitis." Alyssa said, calmly.

"What about it?" Karina suddenly snapped her fingers. "It did this before. You were talking about this."

Loki drew another knife. "You *are* dead." His expression shifted to annoyance. "Your stupid body *adapted* to being dead, and decided you can inhabit it while dead. You don't train your magic. Your magic learns from experience. That's why you suddenly were able to defend yourself against my knife."

Lightning struck me, and very briefly everything went entirely bright around us.

I stepped closer to him.

"Wow." Loki blinked. "Now *that* is magic."

Everything felt painful, but I felt like me again.

"Did she just-" Alyssa began.

"Pretty sure Death isn't going to like that." Karina grumbled.

I didn't respond. I didn't think. I just acted.

My hand drew my gun, and there was a loud thunder crack as I pulled the trigger.

Loki fell to the ground.

"Impossible." He whispered.

I spun about, and fired again.

The first Loki vanished, and the Loki now before me looked surprised, falling backwards with a gut wound.

"You're ready." He said, with a laugh. "Soon, the others will be, too."

He froze solid, and fell into a pile of ice.

"Is he dead?" Alyssa asked.

"Is Harmony?" Karina asked.

"Fair point." Alyssa admitted.

Karina checked her phone, and blinked.

"Harmony?" She asked.

"What?" I turned, finally breaking out of the angry trance.

She held up her phone.

"They're... not dead." Karina blinked. "The cases don't even exist."

"This wasn't real?" Alyssa frowned.

"It was what could be real." I clarified.

"What do you mean?" Karina looked back down at her phone.

"What could be real?"

"If magic continues to seep into this world." I added.

The three of us were silent after that.

The sun had set.

"If Harmony died-" Alyssa began.

"It would have stayed." I shook my head. "I don't think he intended to undo it."

"You think you forced his hand." Karina scrunched up her face. "That makes a kind of sense. You fired something magic at him. It's just possible there was an unexpected interaction."

"Because you saved Vince?" Alyssa asked.

"Honestly, we have no real way of knowing." Karina sighed. "This isn't magic we have in the books."

"You'll get a hell of a promotion when you write that book." Alyssa's tone was more dry than the Afghanistan deserts.

"Are you MAD? I can't write about this." Karina scoffed. "This is INSANE. Nobody will take it seriously."

"What about your report?" Alyssa countered.

"Be honest." I said, calmly. "Every. Word."

Karina gave me an uncertain look. "You realize that if I do that, you might find yourself in an uncomfortable position with military intelligence."

"Listen, if *The Norse God of Treachery* finds her intolerable, do you honestly think the CFNIS intelligence department has a chance?" Alyssa scoffed.

"You're the one who said that intellectual equals were astonishingly uncommon, there." I added.

Karina squinted, before raising her eyebrows. "You think they *need* to know this."

"I think the world is going to get even crazier than it already is, and the only government agency that's on the side of trying to save this world from the crazy fish hooks we're about to see probably should know what they're up against." I nodded.

"This isn't about Harmony." Alyssa laughed. "This is about protecting."

"That *is* sort of her thing, isn't it?" Karina admitted.

"Safe." I gave Alyssa a smirk.

"I'd say we need a drink, but I'm not sure there's anything strong enough for this." Alyssa shook her head.

"Ink. Truer words, I've never heard." Karina chuckled.

"Well, I should hope so." I paused, before giving a mischievous smirk. "There is a truth field, after all."

"Oh, Guppy. That's a terrible joke."

"Okay, but you laughed."

"I did not."

"You wanted to."

"Shut up."

Epilogue

March 16th, 2020

Richmond Naval base, Richmond, British Columbia

Oh, hey, it's this jerk again.

I stepped into my office after my traditional morning run.

I almost began changing back into my uniform, before I realized there was someone already in my office.

"Uh." I cleared my throat, before recognizing the scent. "Captain Gallagher."

"So." The Captain crossed his arms. "You tripped across a trickster, and your first thought was to try and bite him to death?"

"Listen, I did try shooting them prior to that point." I pointed out.

Gallagher nodded. "I read the report." He frowned. "The entirely unredacted, nothing held back report. That's a dangerous practice."

"I swore an oath, once." I retorted. "I can't help protect if others don't know what's going on. Look at how this case turned out."

Gallagher stared at me sternly, and there was nearly a full minute of silence as the two of us stared each other down.

"Fair point." He admitted. "Karina needed to know. The others, too. The only people on this team that aren't scratched by this are Chief Petty Officer Zaheer and Doctor Zehlendorf."

"Oh, it affected them." I paused. "It's probably for the best that they don't recall it."

"They don't?" Gallagher looked puzzled.

"Do you?" I pointed out.

He fell silent again.

I shrugged. "I asked them. They don't seem to remember anything." I took a moment. "Jill, in particular."

"Small blessings, then." He paused. "Best thank whatever god that was looking after them."

"I don't have to. We're very familiar with each other." Neither of us could keep a straight face for very long.

"I cannot believe how *absolutely ridiculous* this case file is." He paused just long enough to point at me. "Or you are."

"You're telling me? I've LITERALLY died twice in the past month." I shot back.

"You got better." He tried to keep a laugh back.

"That's up for debate. I got half better, at least."

That was it.

There was no holding back the laughter.

Maybe this guy wasn't so bad after all.

Some kind of nature

Four of us sat, staring at the graves behind Granddad's house.

Granddad sipped tea.

Alyssa and Karina sipped coffee.

I was drinking vodka straight out of the bottle.

We had been silent, just staring at the graves, lost in our own thoughts.

"You had the chance to bring her back." Karina said, fixing her gaze on Lauren's grave.

"She had the chance to bring my grandmother back." Alyssa added.

Karina looked down, and rubbed a hand along her legs.

"Why didn't you?" Granddad asked.

"Human nature." Karina paused, then winced. "Well. Not quite."

"Harmony isn't wired that way." Alyssa added. "You should know."

The four of us fell silent once more.

"How much would it have cost?" Granddad asked, barely above a whisper.

"Too much." A familiar voice said, from behind us.

Althaia stepped between us, to stare at the tombstones. "Alena would be proud."

"Her father, too." Granddad said, after a moment's thought.

"He wanted her to fight his way." Karina paused to sip her drink. "Except his way included a truly incredible amount of unnecessary people dying."

"And manipulating people into playing his game with their deaths." Alyssa added.

"And if there's one thing you would never do." Granddad chuckled. "You'd never condone an innocent dying for an agenda."

"Funny thing coming from a soldier." Althaia added with just a hint of judgement.

"She isn't a soldier." Alyssa retorted.

"She's the Guardian, now." Karina paused. "And if there's anything I've come to understand about her, it's that there is absolutely nothing that she's going to tolerate threatening people while she's around."

"I should hope not." Granddad chuckled. "That's how she came to have such a fantastic family, after all."

"How so?" Karina blinked.

"Ask Vince." I paused. "And Jill. And Doctor Zehlendorf."

"And me." Alyssa added.

Karina laughed. "You know? I'm glad I met you."

"Not half as glad as I am to have met you." I gave her a peaceful smile and nod.

"If you two are done." Althaia frowned. "I came to say goodbye."

"Goodbye?" I looked up at her sharply.

"Well. You've been drawing my magic out." She paused. "And healing you from death took too much of my life force. I'm afraid I won't be around to save you, next time."

"I don't understand." I scrunched up my face.

"Do not cry, little fish." Althaia patted my head gently. "This was the whole point."

"What was?" Karina looked like she was about to cry. "You intended to die?"

"No." Althaia shook her head. "I intended to protect the world."

There was a crack of thunder, and it began to rain.

A bright flash of lightning struck where she stood.

And she was gone.

The four of us sat in the rain in silence, and then Granddad got up. He returned shortly with a couple of two by fours.

He withdrew a pocket knife from his belt, and began etching out the name *Althaia* into the wood.

And we sat in the rain, sipping our increasingly watered down drinks.

The last honor guard for The Mysterious Healing Song.

Captain Salisbury frowned as the two of us stood in front of him and a man wearing Canadian Forces Provost Marshal rank insignias who I didn't recognize.

"Our judicial review is complete." The CFPM said, quietly.

"What judicial review?" Doctor Zehlendorf asked, from beside me.

"You were both reduced in rank during a previous incident for separate reasons." Salisbury paused. "Your recent conduct has called into question the judgement of the officer who filed the complaints against you, particularly in contrast to his own conduct."

"The decision of the judicial review requested by your commanding officer, Captain Gallagher, is complete." The CFPM added, clarifying.

"Ah." Zehlendorf paused. "I see."

"I'm glad it doesn't have to be spelled out for you." The CFPM paused. "It is the decision of this review panel that you both are to have the incident in question struck from your record, and your previous rank restored. Commander Williams, as you currently hold that position, and a secondary judicial review of your conduct surrounding the joint case with the Gambling Enforcement Agency has been similarly resolved."

"What does that mean, exactly?" Zehlendorf asked.

The General held out two silver boxes.

"You wear them proudly." He paused. "You two seem to know what they are for."

I opened the box, and turned to Doctor Zehlendorf with a raised eyebrow.

"Thank you, Provost Marshal." I said, with a nod.

"And you, Captain Salisbury." Doctor Zehlendorf paused.

"And you, Captain Zehlendorf." I did my best to keep a straight face.

"And you, Captain Williams." Doctor Zehlendorf nodded.

Salisbury winced. "I am going to regret signing off on this."

"So, do we call you Alfonso, now?" I asked.

"Hey Al, are you watching your cholesterol?" Doctor Zehlendorf added.

"I hate you both with the burning passion of 7,000 suns." Salisbury grumbled.

"I'm taking this as having no further business. You are all dismissed." The Provost Marshal paused, trying to keep a straight face. "Captains. Good day." He added, with just the slightest smirk.

"Who is that guy?" I whispered to Salisbury, as we left.

"That's the new Provost Marshal. There was a big press release." Salisbury sounded surprised by my ignorance.

"I don't really watch television." I retorted.

"That is Captain Provost Marshal Vanille." Salisbury took a moment. "I'm surprised you don't recognize your ex-father-in-law."

"I never met him." I froze in place. "That's Victor's dad?"

"Indeed, Captain." Salisbury gave a bemused look. "And you have gone out of your way to draw his attention to you."

I closed my eyes and swore in German.

"Gesundheit." Doctor Zehlendorf retorted.

Salisbury began to chuckle, and then he walked away from the two of us in a full roaring laugh.

"Captain Salisbury has a sense of humor?" Doctor Zehlendorf asked.

"Apparently." I shook my head. "Well. That's someone I'm not sure I want to have access to my black file."

"You're presuming he didn't already have access to it." Zehlendorf laughed. "Regardless, he seemed genuinely happy about this."

"Victor would have liked it."

"So would his Granddaughter."

"Of that, I have no doubt."

Captains Harmony Williams, Alfred Zehlendorf, Leftenants Karina Gill and Alyssa Sanchez and Chief Petty Officers Zilla "Jill" Zaheer and Vincent LaSenza will return in

Guardian Harmony: Swan song

A cold case haunts the team as a new body forces them to work with others who tried to catch the same serial killer 5 years prior.

Leaving their victims *steamed* to death, with no forensic evidence left behind, "The Steam Clock Killer" haunts both Alfred Zehlendorf, and Frank Gillard.

Except.

Frank is dead already, and it would seem that the good doctor isn't far behind him.
(Guest starring the Fae Noir cast)
((Obviously))